The Crystal Ballroom

Also by Libby Sommer and published by Ginninderra Press
My Year With Sammy

Libby Sommer

The Crystal Ballroom

Acknowledgements

Versions of 'Henry', 'Tom', 'Keirin', 'Michael', 'The Spa' and 'Tango' were first published in *Quadrant*.

Thank you to my mentors Nell Dunn, Amanda Lohrey, Joyce Kornblatt and Jan Cornall for support and encouragement, particularly in the early years of my writing journey. And thank you to all the feedback groups I've attended during my writing apprenticeship. Your feedback has been, and continues to be, essential to my development as a writer.

Thank you to the Literature Board of the Australia Council for two emerging writers grants for new work that enabled me to keep writing.

The Crystal Ballroom
ISBN 978 1 76041 327 9
Copyright © text Libby Sommer 2017
Cover image © Forewer

First published 2017 by
GINNINDERRA PRESS
PO Box 3461 Port Adelaide 5015
www.ginninderrapress.com.au

Contents

This book is dedicated to my children Steven, Craig and Erika.

Henry

Ingrid doesn't have children. She says she's much too selfish for all of that. She's always preferred dogs. When people tell me the problems they have with their children, I'm pleased I don't have any, she likes to say.

We are drinking coffee at my place and, as usual, I am telling her all about it, telling her what happened that first time with Henry. Do you want the long version or should I keep it short?

Give me the details, she says. It's intriguing.

Well, he arrived at my door on a Friday night. I've got the lights down low so I don't see him clearly at first. I'm standing at the top of the stairs waiting, when a person with long hair, trousers and a jacket emerges. At first I think I've let a strange woman into the building by mistake. As the person gets closer, I realise it's Henry, with his hair out – although he seems different. His thick dark brown hair is freshly washed and blow-dried – puffy – you know how it is when you've just washed your hair? It hangs to his shoulders. The other times it was tied back in a ponytail, or twisted up into a bun at the back of his head.

What's wrong? he says.

Nothing, I answer, still in shock that I thought he was a woman.

I keep the lights down low, so I don't notice his shoes. He kicks them off before we sit down on the couch.

What's the matter? he says.

He's kissing me on the lips and I notice a slightly sour smell. He has this nice way of kissing – gently, very sweet usually. And he makes a little sighing sound every now and again.

I'm smelling the shampoo in his hair near my face and tasting the slightly acrid flavour of him. Is he nervous? I'm kissing him and running my hand over his chest. It's then that I feel a lump, like a breast, although it feels spongy.

He's got breasts? Ingrid exclaims.

No. I knew he didn't have breasts. He's wearing a bra. A stuffed bra, and a lace silk camisole.

Oh, no!

Who have I let into my apartment? What sort of a crazy is he? I know nothing about him, apart from the fact that he's a great dancer and a good kisser. What's going on? I ask.

What do you mean?

What was that I felt?

What did it feel like?

So then I notice his feet are covered by stockings. I look over to his shoes by the side of the room. Black strappy sandals with a small heel.

Are you wearing stockings? I ask. And a suspender belt?

That's when I want him to leave. I'm so repulsed with the possibility of seeing him in a suspender belt and stockings.

Did you say that to him? Ingrid asks.

No. But he could tell. He offered to go.

So, what happened?

Well, dinner's cooking – I don't want to waste the food, you know what I'm like – so I stand up and go into the kitchen. I boil up some pasta and warm up a tomato and spinach sauce I've made already – he's a vegetarian – and then serve it up in bowls and bring them to the coffee table, him watching me closely, while clutching a cushion from the lounge to his stomach, every now and then making a hiccup kind of noise, as if catching his breath.

I want you to know early on, he says. The last woman I went out with… I told her after eighteen months and she walked straight out. Why shouldn't I have silk next to my body? It feels nice. Why shouldn't I wear high heels to make me taller? Women wear men's clothes. Why not the reverse?

Do you feel like a woman? I ask. A woman in a man's body?'

Do you know what it feels like to be a man? he snaps. I'm not someone you'd take to the family barbecue, he adds.

Have you been in long relationships with women who've accepted it? I ask.

Yes, he says. I make a good friend. I love shopping. I'm a good one to take shopping. When I go out in a dress and high heels around my way, no one bats an eyelid.

Does he use a condom? Ingrid puts in.

Yes. Always.

Make sure it doesn't come off. Don't have sex with him any more.

He's a fabulous dancer.

Just dance with him, then.

A little later, when I take the bowls to the kitchen, he puts on some music. I'd asked him to bring CDs. He's very fussy about what he listens to.

Has he been married? Ingrid asks.

For two years. She left him for another woman.

Ingrid giggles. What's the world coming to? she says.

I don't want you to judge him, Ingrid.

I'm not. But he's confused. He doesn't know what he is. You shouldn't get involved with someone like that. If you're in an intimate relationship, you take in the other person's stuff. You must know that? It passes across from one person to the other.

It's true, he's confused. But I really like him.

Just dance with him. That's all.

I said to him early on, when we seemed to get on well and to have so much in common, that I'd like to see him regularly.

Is he seeing anyone else?

I asked him that. His response was, I'm with you at this moment, and have been for the last few hours.

He's probably seeing someone else.

The main thing is that he's not into men. He laughed when I asked him if he's on hormones. I'm just me, he said. I've got nice legs, though. It's horrible being me, he added. It's an awful thing to live with. He gave a massive, heart-rending sigh.

Someone like him would find it hard to get a woman, Ingrid says.

It's probably hopeless anyway. He's eighteen years younger than me – apart from anything else.

Another short-lived relationship, she says, unable to disguise the disapproval in her voice. You need an older man, more of a father figure.

Speak for yourself.

She shrugs. Does his family know?

No. He said his mother might suspect something.

So it's his secret – he lives a secret life, Ingrid says, but I can see she doesn't understand.

I'm upset. But I'm not going to talk about it with her any more. I know what she thinks.

So, what else? Ingrid says. What else happened?

Nothing else. That's it. We ate dinner and then he went home.

I look around the room where Henry and I sat, see the black timber painted floor, the bright cushions on the chairs, the colourful paintings on the walls, the photos of myself and the children on the mantelpiece, the *New Yorker* magazines he'd flipped through still there on the coffee table.

You don't remember what it's like being single, I say to Ingrid at the front door.

Gary

Ingrid and I are lying on beach towels on the grass down near the water, sipping iced tea.

'Are your two fellows called Larry and Gary?' Ingrid asks in her precisely articulated English voice. 'Or was I mishearing something?'

'Yes, it's funny, isn't it? Larry rang the other night and I said, "Who?" I wasn't sure if he'd said Gary or Larry. They're not really my two guys, though. Either one of them could disappear in a puff of smoke. I haven't seen Larry for ages. Another workaholic. It's a shame…we dance so well together.'

We watch as mothers, their faces tightened in concentration, rub suntan lotion on the necks and backs of their children. A pontoon in the middle of the pool sways on the current. Two boys dangle their feet in the cooling water. Children jump off the platform into the harbour, although some of them are pushed. That's exactly what I need. A good shove. I stay on the edge for far too long.

'What does Larry do?' Ingrid asks lazily.

'He has his own business. Something to do with computers and the internet. He rings, but never makes any plans to get together to dance. He seems to work twenty-four-seven.'

Ingrid finishes her tea and lies back on the towel. Her new lemon bikini highlights flawless brown skin. She loves her bikinis, even though her body shape has changed so much over the years. She's not what you'd call fat, but her waist seems to have disappeared. Not that I can talk. I'm playing it safe in a black one-piece hoping to hide the rolls. Are they skin folds or fat rolls? Creases or love handles? The metabolism changes as we get older – it's all so hard. At least we're still ballroom dancing.

Ingrid takes off her square-shaped black glasses and her face softens.

'From what you've told me, I don't think Gary adds anything to your life. It's better to spend time with people who love you.'

I look over to the children digging holes in the sand near the edge of the water, protected from the sun by their fluoro Cancer Council tops and wonder who loves me. My children?

I notice the bronzed older women around the same age as us exposing their necks and faces to the sun, hatless and topless, one woman so gaunt, she looks like a holocaust survivor.

'So what about this Gary fellow then?' Ingrid says rolling on to her stomach. 'How old is he?'

'My age. The thing is, he has no social skills. He doesn't speak properly. I don't think he can read.'

'Stamp it out quickly!' Ingrid says authoritatively. 'If one of the good dancers sees you holding hands, they'll assume you're a couple and not invite you to dance. Anyway, that's far too forward of him to be holding your hand when you've just met.'

'When he walks me out to my car, I kiss him goodbye on the cheek but he wants a kiss on the lips.'

Ingrid nods, then sits up and opens her pack of cigarettes. 'I'm going to have to have a smoke. Do you mind if I do it here, or do you want me to move?'

'That's fine.'

She manages to light up despite the wind blowing in from the sea. 'Men like Gary become a burden. You don't need it. It's better to have no regular dance partner. I think I'm right in saying that we both enjoy the challenge of dancing with different guys.' She inhales deeply then turns her face away to exhale. 'Tell him you feel very lucky to have been dancing with a competition dance partner like him, but it stops there. You're not interested in anything else to do with him.'

In the distance, a ferry passes in front of the haze of grey city buildings and I picture Gary with his thick gold necklace and matching linked bracelet. On his fingers are large rings and in his ear a diamond stud. He's dressed in black trousers and a dark top and has with him another shirt that he leaves in the men's room ready to change into halfway through the dance when he is drenched with sweat. Not all the men do this, so in the progressives they're slippery and smelly and it's best not to breathe in for a few seconds when it's your turn to dance with them.

'You won't ask me to take my diamond stud out, will you?' Gary once asked.

I told him that it looks good. It sparkles in the light.

'I used to compete in dressage at the Easter Show and I have some photos to prove it.'

'You like to do everything well?'

He smiled. 'Is that a bad thing?'

'No, it's good.'

The pool is surrounded by a boardwalk of wooden planks and trimmed with a white railing. A boy in long loose board shorts jumps off the edge. Next moment his feet are above the water joined at the ankles, his toes spread wide like splayed flippers. Close to the shore a boy falls backwards into the sea with a shout of delight.

'I don't know how other women manage to do it,' I say to Ingrid. 'To just keep them as a dance partner. Are Hannah and Gavin on together? I noticed he had his hand on her thigh when they sat at our table last time.'

'Gavin? The fatso? No. She said they're not.'

'It certainly looks like something's going on.'

'She must be giving him a little bit.'

'A little bit?'

In front of us, two men lie face down, their feet playing footsies. They've taken turns to use a spray can to cover their perfectly toned bodies with oil. A sharp citrus smell hovers in the air as Ingrid and I move on to more gossip about the Crystal Ballroom dancers.

I tell her that I'd asked Larry if Diane and Bill are an item but he'd said they're not. 'They look like they are,' I said. 'He told me they aren't. "Bill and I share Diane," he said. He grinned, then added, "For dancing, that is."'

Ingrid laughs.

A splash as another boy runs along and jumps from the wooden perimeter of the pool.

'You know Henry?' I say. 'The one with the ponytail who likes to dress as a woman?'

'Yes. I remember him.'

'On the phone the other night he said he thinks of himself as a male lesbian. He'd happily be a woman, but because he looks more like a man and because he fancies women, he's a male lesbian.'

'That's funny.' Ingrid covers her handbag with a towel and uses it as a pillow. 'The whole gender role thing.'

People in wide-brimmed hats stroll along the promenade between the grass where we lie on the sand of the beach.

'Years ago I read an article about a woman who was diagnosed with breast cancer and it was the story of her journey to remission. The only thing I remember is that as soon as she received the diagnosis, she told each of her two lovers.'

'Two lovers?' Ingrid frowns. 'So what's wrong with us?'

'There's nothing wrong with us. We're doing all right.'

'No need to get angry. It was only a joke.'

'It's not a joke. It's not funny. Anyway, you're married. You've got a partner. A warm body in the bed every night.'

'Farting and snoring.'

'Nothing's perfect.'

Outside the harbour pool, yachts with sails of blue, white and grey and speed boats with brightly painted hulls bob at anchor.

I hear myself sigh. 'The thing is, some people choose lives of colour and movement while others choose safety and security. That's what I heard someone say on the radio.'

Ingrid shrugs before standing up and wrapping herself in a flowered sarong. 'Let's go up to the café and have an ice cream.'

'Choose your spot,' says the waitress.

We decide on one of the small square tables with fake marble tops under a canvas umbrella where we can look out across Double Bay.

'This has the best view,' the waitress says. She gives the table a quick wipe then brings us a glass of water each.

'Thank you,' says Ingrid, her photosensitive glasses now a dark grey.

The wind has picked up again and churns the water into little white caps. In front of us the tangerine bougainvillea attracts a bee, or is it a hornet? The seagulls squawk. Waves roll in and break on the hard sand. Another seagull, wings outstretched, glides to a standstill on the pontoon, his movements as smooth as a good heel turn in the foxtrot.

'They've forecast thunderstorms for this afternoon.'

'Really?'

Ingrid has ordered an ice cream and I'm drinking an iced coffee. Her meticulous fingers edge the tight wrapper down the cone. 'My nails are so strong I could use them as a screwdriver.'

'How do you keep them like that?'

'You know what? I go to bed, paint my nails and watch TV.' She takes another delicate bite from the nut and chocolate studded rim of her ice cream.

'Gary measured me up for size that first time. He asked me how tall I am. That's when he said he was looking for a new partner for comp.'

'Dancing comp is a big commitment in terms of time and money.' She shakes her head. 'A big sacrifice. You have to have private lessons several times a week.'

'Maybe I'd like it.'

Down near the water a seagull struts along the path by the sand his tender neck curved like an S-bend. It's hard to achieve a body arch like that in ballroom – to be able to shape your back by pulling up and out from the waist. The gull stops abruptly and gazes out to sea, stands there where the sea slaps the shore and watches. Watches and waits. And waits.

'Gary said he paid for all the lessons with his old dance partner, but I'd want to pay for myself,' I continue. 'They spent a lot of time together going to the comps and putting in all that training. I asked him if they had more than a dance relationship, but he said they didn't. He said she wanted it but he didn't.'

The leaves of the bougainvillea flicker in the wind.

'She's older than him. That's Gary's reason. He said she turned up on his doorstep at three in the morning more than once. He told her she could sleep on the couch. So he says. She won't speak to him now. He reckons he doesn't know why. He said he's done so much for her. Paid for all the lessons, helped her in her business and then she goes and asks some scum to dance with her at one of the comps. "The bloke wasn't even dressed properly," he said. "In jeans and sneakers. You should have seen him. Not like me. I always dress well. A person has to dress well. It's the most important thing."'

Ingrid licks the ice cream from the inside of the foil wrap as she pulls it back further from the sugar cone.

'Something's still going on there with him and the old dance partner. She made a big scene last Friday when he was dancing with another woman. She went up to him in front of everyone and tried to take him off her. He finally admitted that there was something going on. "Sort of," he said. And he's dancing with her at the socials again. He hovers around near the kitchen so he can be quick to invite her when the next bracket starts up. He never takes his eyes off her. He knows where she is in the room all the time. When he danced rock and roll with me, it was right in front of her. He made sure we were dancing directly in her line of vision.'

'How awful! I'd hate that.' Ingrid wipes the corners of her mouth with a serviette.

The sky has come over all grey although the clouds are still bright with light. A bird calls out, over and over again. An Indian myna hops to a higher branch hoping for a better view of his prey. The sky presses low. The threat of rain drives us off the beach

Flashes of lightning. It cracks the sky. From this new place where I live, I can look down into the harbour towards Shark Island, where yachts are struggling towards the horizon in their twilight race. It's something to look forward to, the way the harbour seems different every day. Red and white and blue triangular sails are becalmed in the windless air. Are they moving at all?

I'm remembering the last time I saw Gary. Ingrid and I were at the Crystal Ballroom and he stood by the door, his hair and face shiny, his shirt damp. It was a hot Friday night in December. He'd been dancing all that day at one of the leagues clubs out west with a woman he said he'd known for a long time. I think he was waiting for her to turn up. I remember the darkness of his clothing, the distracted look in his eyes, his tight lips as he looked around the dance floor, his arrogant, tense bearing, the broadness of his shoulders, and the secretive expression on his face. I know I was conscious of how we looked, Ingrid and I sitting there at the dance with our sweaty red faces and hair plastered to our heads in limp tendrils.

The sky pales to a thick grey with the sound of rolling thunder. The sea darkens and deepens. The yachts on a slow frantic journey home.

I haven't told Ingrid the whole story. I don't want to tell her how it ended. How Gary gave me the flick. Left a message on my answer machine to say he wouldn't be available for any more dancing.

But I did tell Henry – Henry, my friend with a ponytail.

'It's in the DNA,' he said with a knowing snigger. 'Men are programmed that way. If you weren't prepared to give him what he wanted, why waste his time? He went off to look elsewhere.'

The weather envelops the window and closes in.

Caleb

Sofia reached for the steering wheel lock and clicked it into place. She looked out to the dimly lit street – only the children's playground illuminated by a floodlight. It'll be even darker walking back to the car. She took a deep breath. You've made it this far. Don't turn back now. Only a short walk and you'll be there. Driving across the Anzac Bridge, she'd reminded herself how she enjoyed the excitement of not knowing. The possibility that something unexpected might happen.

She pressed the grey circle on the black disc in her hand and the doors snapped closed. It gave her great pleasure, this little remote control. That and her automatic garage door. Things were definitely improving.

As she passed the suburban families eating on the pavement, she did her best to look inconspicuous in her short lace see-through dress and high heels. She tugged at the hem of her skirt, pulling it down towards her knees. If I see anyone I know, I'll die.

She found the place pretty easily. Well, she'd been there before, but not for a long time. The Crystal Ballroom. The words were written in large letters above the doorway of the old movie theatre, an elaborate 1920s Flemish-style building with entry doors set back into the facade and window openings shaped in beautiful semicircular arches. It was wedged between a 'my mac' store on the left and 'sushi sushi' on the right. The big curved entry arches faced the street where three large green bins labelled 'trade waste' lay in wait to be emptied beside an overturned plastic milk crate. A motorbike leant against the 'no standing' sign.

She walked through the heavy black wrought-iron doors and across the marble entry foyer to a man sitting behind a glass and chrome desk in the reception area.

'Do you want to see my membership card?'

'Yes,' he said from under the huge crystal chandelier that lit up the shiny black planter boxes, studded leather couches and plaster-cast figurines.

It was the biggest chandelier she'd ever seen, but not quite as large as she remembered it.

'It's a long time since you were here last.' The man behind the desk smiled.

Musty. The smell drifted down the grand curved staircase and landed in the foyer ready to engulf anyone bold enough to enter.

Frank Sinatra's voice crooned upstairs and a soft ripple made its way down through her body. Better that than sitting at a desk moving numbers around all day or lying on the couch in front of the television.

'No expectations,' her friend Ingrid had said. 'Just go for the dancing.'

She climbed the steps, pulling again at the underskirt beneath the lace that kept riding up her body, the delicate fabric catching on the python skin of her bag. She'd bought it in Brazil from the man who'd killed the snake and made the purse. She must remember to oil it more often.

Near the door to the ballroom sat a curly-haired man in suit trousers and white shirt at a trestle table covered by a linen tablecloth. In front of him was a tin money box filled with paper notes and gold coins and a pile of flyers that advertised the dates of the dances. She handed over the fifteen dollars and took a couple of round white peppermints from the ceramic saucer beside him.

Walking in was always the hardest part.

Men and women sat at tables and chairs on the carpeted area that surrounded the 1930s sprung wooden dance floor. On the podium a disc jockey stood behind a long table covered with CDs. A change of tempo and something loud and fast filled the room from the stereo system. No poker machines here.

She noticed an interesting-looking man with longish hair, blond and gelled back, his skin a golden olive, alone at a table on the other side of the room. Perhaps he was one of those rock and rollers with hair in the style of the fifties, slicked-back.

She decided to make her way in his general direction after buying a drink. I'll feel better with a drink in my hand. For a moment, she couldn't remember the position of the bar. Was it to the left or to the right? Christ, where is it?

'Soda water, no ice,' she said to the girl with the smooth face and a ponytail.

'Lemon?'

'Thanks.'

They smiled at each other. Sofia wondered whether the girl made judgements about the people who came to functions like this. Singles dances. Not a real dance. Not somewhere where everyone knew how to do the steps.

Balloons in reds and greens hung from the ceiling, their tails curly and dangling, but not low enough to brush her in the face as she manoeuvred her way between the tables and chairs, skimming past the men and women waiting for something to happen. She sat down on one of the chairs lined up against the wall, hoping the man next to her wouldn't think that she'd walked all the way across the room to sit next to him. She perched on the edge of the seat with her back partly towards him. Not that she had anything against the man. It was just that she didn't want to get bogged down with polite conversation and then she'd be stuck.

'Don't I know you?' he asked.

Oh yes, she thought to herself. I've heard that one before. She turned to him. Saw his thin face and receding wispy hair. 'I don't know. You do look a bit familiar, I must say.'

'What's your name?'

'Sofia.'

'Yes, I do know you. You rented an office next to mine at Blackwater Bay.'

She remembered him now. He was into numerology and feng shui. Told her she had her table in the wrong position in the room. Not that it helped; she still spent most days with the door closed lying on the couch watching the ceiling fan go around.

'Yes, that's right. But I've forgotten your name.'

'Sam. So how's the stock market treating you?'

'The same as everyone else,' she answered. 'We're all hurting. So tell me, how's the book coming along?'

He went on at great length about his ideas for a book on feng shui as Latin music pumped and pulsated around them.

The dance floor filled with swaying hips and Cuban heels, as couples moved towards and then away from each other to the rhythm of the beat.

Sofia found it hard to concentrate on what Sam was saying. She'd been trying to keep an eye on the people seated in front and on the dance floor, and the blond man with the gelled-back hair opposite, but she felt a certain obligation to keep eye contact with Sam.

He stopped talking, his legs slightly apart, his elbows resting on his knees. They stayed in silence for a time. A group of women in short skirts and fishnets sat down next to the blond man. She wondered if he'd remain unattached for long.

She felt Sam watching her, waiting for her to say something.

'Do you come to dances like this very often?' he asked.

'No. It's much easier to stay at home,' she sighed into her drink. 'What about you?'

'I've been learning ballroom dancing so I go to quite a few now. Cammeray Golf Club on a Friday night is one of my favourites. The women there are friendly. At least they'll dance with you when you ask them.'

Sofia nodded and took a sip of soda water.

'I don't see too many women here asking men to dance, though,' he added. 'They should.'

When another Latin number filled the room, Sofia decided she might as well give him a go. 'Can you salsa?' she asked, gesturing towards the dancing.

'Sort of.'

'It's all in the rhythm,' she instructed, taking both his hands in hers on the dance floor. Rough hands. She inhaled a whiff of something familiar, probably Brut. She stepped back, giving them both room to move, not wedged up close and not too far apart.

A South American man's voice issued saucily from the CD player.

She closed her eyes, relaxing into the music and the seductive sound that seemed to reach from the stereo into her very being. The feeling eased down through her like a shot of whisky drunk straight from the bottle. Loosening up, moving easy.

She was pleased she'd worn her new chorus line shoes from Bloch's with the ankle strap so she was secure as her feet twisted in a kick ball change to the syncopated beat. No problem, not like keeping those stupid sling backs on, having to clutch them with your toes.

By the end of the dance she was flushed with the heat, and beads of perspiration had collected along Sam's forehead. He'd turned out to be a capable dancer. She excused herself and went into the ladies to mop up.

On the way she complained to the man at the door about how hot it was in the room and he told her they had plans to change venues in future.

'We're fed up with the lousy air conditioning too,' he said. 'But the people who run this place won't do anything about it.'

On her frequent trips to the bathroom to cool down, two different women told her they'd been watching her dance. The second woman asked if that was the rumba. Of course it was, what did she think? But the woman used the question to show Sofia her own version. Demonstrated right there in the hallway outside the toilets. This big woman swinging her hips from side to side showing how she could do it.

'Where did you learn to dance?' the woman who could rumba asked.

'At Drummoyne Dance Studio. With Frank Pauls.'

'Frank Pauls? That bastard!'

'What do you mean?'

'After what he did to his wife.'

'Frank Pauls? He's gay. He can't be married. He's not into women as far as I know.'

But now that she thought about it, Sofia remembered Frank telling her about an affair with a black female American dancer. Strange. Seems some gays can have a bit both ways. Which reminded her of last Friday night after work at the cocktail party when she chatted to the two cooks. One straight and one gay. She fancied the gay cook, whose name was Rupert. He was open and friendly and the two of them hit it off straight away. They got into a deep and meaningful conversation as if they'd known each other for years.

'I live with my partner,' Rupert had said. 'He's a playwright.'

'Really? And what about you? Have you always been a cook?'

'No, not at all. I used to be a sculptor. Now I design food. I'm still creating with my hands.'

'The food is excellent by the way. Especially those little salmon and goat cheese tarts.'

'They're my speciality.'

'Where did you meet your partner?' she asked, accepting another mini tart from the tray.

'Through an ad in a gay newspaper.'

Sofia was fascinated. It's something she was always wondering about. How do people meet?

'I placed an ad once too,' she said.

'You and I believe in the numbers game. Increasing the odds.'

'Exactly.'

She was just about to tell him funny stories about some of the guys she'd met from the ad when the other cook joined them and they changed the subject.

Rupert stood behind her to point to an attractive man on the other side of the room. The man's mop of black curls sat atop close-cropped sides. Rupert pressed up close to line the man up in her line of vision, so close his chin touched the top of her head. She could feel herself going red in the face when she felt the pressure of his body against her back.

Later, the straight cook said that Rupert had sex with women from time to time. 'He's okay about the oyster. That he can handle. But breasts! That's something else. You'd have to cover them up.' And the straight cook demonstrated, folding his arms tightly against his chest as if he was hugging himself.

Bind my breasts? That wouldn't be an option. To be bound and gagged.

'The Frank Pauls I know isn't married,' Sofia repeated now to the woman who demonstrated the rumba in the hallway outside the ladies toilets.

The woman shrugged. 'I was married to a dance teacher once.' Remembered love filled her face before she laughed bitterly, showing a criss-cross of discoloured and jagged lower teeth. 'He was tall and handsome as well.'

So she too had a husband once. Also tall dark and handsome. Not that Sofia's could dance. She smiled at the woman. 'That's what's so good about coming to these dances. It helps to fill the gaps.'

'All we need is someone to dance with.'

'I guess there are worse things to be dependent on than needing a dance partner.'

'Dancing is better than sex. You'd agree with that, I'm sure.'

'If you can get the right partner, dancing is magic. There's nothing else like it.'

'A good strong leader. That's not too much to ask for, is it?' laughed the woman. 'Then you can be swept away. Let go. Become the perfect follower.'

'You must have had lots of that with your husband, the dance teacher?'

'That's what I miss the most.'

'Being transported to another world?'

'You've got it.'

'Every woman's dream,' Sofia sighed wistfully. 'To be with a man who can dance.' She gestured towards the ballroom with its stained-glass windows. She wanted to get back inside, where the real action was happening.

The chandeliers, positioned along the length of the room, with only the occasional missing light bulb, lit up the rows of liquor bottles lining the shelves of the bar. With soda water in hand, Sofia watched the dancers. It was an old habit not to drink when she danced. But that was real dancing. Real dancers didn't want to screw up their timing.

From across the room, a man dressed in tangerine shirt and pale calico trousers, who she had noticed before, gave her the nod. He looked reasonable – not too old, regular features, full head of hair. Not bad. The DJ had put on 'Come Over to My Place'.

Unfortunately, the man had no sense of rhythm. He jumped around too fast to the beat, so Sofia had to steer him off the floor after the first dance.

He walked her to his table. 'What would you like to drink?'

'I'm fine, thanks. I've got a soda water at the bar.'

'Go on,' he encouraged. 'Have a glass of wine. It's good to have a drink. That's how I relax, with a drink in my hand.'

'Oh, all right then. I suppose so.' What the hell. One glass won't hurt.

He pulled a chair out to make a place for her and went to the bar.

The only problem was, she'd broken two of her own rules. Never accept a drink, and don't sit down. She didn't want to feel obligated and if you did sit down, you stayed there. Much harder to get up, to summon the courage to put yourself out there again.

He made his way back through the over-heated room and the heaving mass of dancers, bopping to the Beach Boys' 'Barbara Ann'. A glass of Chardonnay for her and a Scotch on the rocks for him.

His name was Brad. Sofia encouraged him to talk. Maybe she'd find they had something in common. She thought he could be Polish with his thick accent and square face.

Brad, who seemed relieved to be able to speak about himself, placed a bony ankle over his knee and pulled at a tangerine silk sock with an equally bony hand. He told her he was a builder and lived down south. 'I like to play soccer when I'm not working. But I'm new to these singles dances. I only split up with my girlfriend three weeks ago.'

'Saturday nights can be pretty lonely when you're not used to it,' she said with empathy in her tone.

He explained at length why it hadn't worked out with his girlfriend. 'Now I miss her,' he said. 'Although she isn't the sort of person I'd want to marry.'

The woman who'd demonstrated the rumba outside the ladies toilets walked past and ruffled Brad's hair in an overly familiar way. He looked like a cocky with his hair sticking straight in the air, so Sofia had to point it out to him. It did look rather ridiculous but then a couple of minutes later, the woman walked back from the opposite direction and did the same thing. Ruffled his hair. Sofia had to tell him, impress on him, because he was reluctant to do anything about it, that his hair was once again standing on end and it would be a good idea to flatten it.

He reached up and smoothed it down and forward across his scalp. 'I don't even know that woman,' he said. 'She asked me to dance. She's not really my type. I liked dancing with her, though. She's good.'

Another bloke tapped Sofia on the shoulder and asked her up. He wore dark blue jeans and a collarless denim shirt with highly polished black leather shoes on his feet.

'Excuse me,' she said to the Polish guy. She stood up, pulling at the sides of her skirt. 'I'll be back soon.'

On the dance floor, she was unpleasantly surprised to find this man was more interested in pulling her up close every couple of seconds to the rhythm of a samba than getting into any real dancing. He kept bumping her chest against his body as he pulled her in with his arms. She didn't find him at all attractive but had hoped he could dance. When he asked her the second time, she said no thanks, she was too hot.

The blond guy with the slicked-back hair, who she'd noticed when she first came in, and the woman who could rumba, danced together. Sofia couldn't help but notice the position of his hand resting on her ample hips, slightly more down towards her bottom than was necessary. He wasn't moving much, so she couldn't tell if he could dance or not, but his handsome face was against the woman's hair. The number ended and the two of them sat down together.

A few minutes later, the blond man stood up and headed towards the door of the ballroom. Sofia excused herself and headed out after him. He stood near the grand staircase smoking. She waited until he finished and then moved towards the entrance door at the same time as he did, as if by chance.

'A hot night,' she said.

He held the door open for her and smiled. 'Yeah. They should do something about the air conditioning.'

Sofia nodded and picked up a peppermint from the dish on their way back in past the security man, who was keeping an eye on things from the doorway. The music had changed pace to something smooth and slow. The couples moved up close as 'Feelings' gushed through the room.

Sofia stood up the back with the blond man and watched. He leaned back against the wall, reached into his shirt pocket for his cigarettes, put one in the corner of his mouth, lit it and flipped away the match.

Sofia sucked at the peppermint, its smooth surface rolling around her tongue. She turned to him. 'Can you rock and roll?'

He shook his head. 'No. I'm not much good at that.'

'That's a shame. I thought with your slicked-back hair you might be an old rock and roller. Not that you're old. But you know what I mean...'

'Sorry. Never got into that sort of thing.'

Sam came over to say goodbye. She wished him good luck with his feng shui book and waved to him as he walked out.

'I noticed you sitting alone when I first came in,' said Sofia to the blond man.

'Yeah?'

'Then that group of women came and sat down with you. They looked very attractive.'

'More money than they know what to do with. Not for me.'

'Oh?'

He dragged deeply on his cigarette, held it in, then exhaled over his shoulder. 'One of the women must own half of Mosman. Has houses that she rents out. She did well out of the divorce.'

Sofia nodded.

'Where do you live?' he asked.

'In the east. And you?'

'Northern beaches now, but I used to live in Lithgow.'

'Lithgow?'

'I worked in the mines.'

'So you're new to Sydney?'

He blew the smoke out and up towards the balloons. 'No, I lived here before.'

Sofia shifted her weight to the other leg. 'So what sort of work are you doing now?'

'I sell flowers from the markets to shops.' He glanced down at his watch. 'I'm at the markets every morning at four.'

'That's early.'

'I'm back home by six.'

'What do you do for the rest of the day?'

'Go to the beach.'

'Oh, so you're a surfer?'

'No,' he said. 'I just like the beach.' He finished his cigarette and ground it out in the ashtray. 'So how do you spend your time?'

'A bit of this and that. I'm a gambler.'

'That's risky.'

'Stocks and shares.'

'Good with numbers?'

'And I'm a whiz at Sudoku and Ken Ken. Sometimes I'm sitting up in bed at midnight still doing those puzzles.'

He nodded. 'Interesting.' And moved in closer behind her. 'What's your name?'

She could almost feel his breath on her neck. 'Sofia. And yours?'

'Caleb.' He moved a step nearer, his body touching hers lightly.

She looked down at her watch, then up at him. 'I'm going to make a move. Would you walk me to my car?'

Outside the air was heavy with humidity, but the main road was devoid of traffic. She removed her keys from her bag as they walked around the corner, across the road and down towards the park, the street dark and overhung with trees. She stopped in front of a small Honda.

Caleb stepped in close to the car, leaned back slightly on the bonnet and pulled her towards him. He pointed at her keys. 'Put those down. They look lethal.' He kissed her lightly.

She responded gently.

He breathed into her ear. 'Can I come home with you?'

'No.'

'Why not?'

'It's late.'

He released his grip and straightened up. Looked at her. 'What's your telephone number?'

'Do you have a mobile?'

'I didn't bring it. Have you got a pen?'

'No. Have you?'

'Nope.'

'You mean you're into puzzles and stuff and you haven't got a pen?'

She patted her tiny handbag. 'I like to travel light. We can use my lip liner.'

He looked into his pockets for a piece of paper. 'I haven't got anything to write on.'

She tore off the top of the peppermint box and wrote her phone number with the lip pencil. She handed it to him and picked up her keys.

He folded the small piece of cardboard carefully and put it into his wallet. 'You can drop me back to my car. It's just around the corner.'

She unlocked the door with a click of the remote and let him in.

He settled into the passenger seat, reached down for the lever, slid the seat back, tilted it, snapped on the seat belt, settled back with a sigh. 'Take me home with you.'

A CD plays a strange combination of rhythms from a cello, an Irish drum and a didgeridoo. The sound of a bath running, the smell of sandalwood incense.

In the water, all warm and wet, soft and slippery.

A coarse towel dries and dabs at moist skin.

Then, in front of the mirror, back turned to the bed, she rubs moisturiser all over. She glimpses herself, sees the flush still in her cheeks, the ringlets at her neck, the brightness of her eyes. Maybe it's the new light dimmer, or the warmth of the overhead heater, but she sees an aliveness there.

The wool carpet rough underfoot as she walks to the bed, lifts the blankets, gently slides between the sheets.

The smell of freshly laundered linen as she lies back and luxuriates remembering those last few moments when she'd dropped him off at his car, a square-edged grey utility. He'd parked on the main road, so she'd stopped under a bright street light to let him out.

'I've got a pen in my glovebox,' he'd said. 'That lip pencil is all smudged. I'll be back in a minute.'

She watched him cross the road, a lopsided walk with his keys bulging from his belt at the side and his trousers hanging low at the back.

The kiss had been nice, but what the hell! It's not as if he can dance.

She turned the key in the ignition and drove off.

What would Ingrid think she wonders now? Although it's not as if she has to tell Ingrid everything.

'You didn't, did you?' is what Ingrid is sure to say.

Well, she'd had a lot of fun, her feet still sore from the dancing. That's how she always knew she'd had the best time: her body aching with exhaustion, her feet on the verge of blistering.

She stretches out diagonally across the bed, wriggles her toes and sinks down into the pillows with a sigh.

Aravind

It was just after eight on a Friday night when I finally arrived at the Crystal Ballroom again. I'd spent ages driving around trying to find somewhere to park. So when I did locate a spot way down Bishops Road, I rang Aravind on the mobile to say I'd be late.

He was still caught up in traffic. He blamed the rain. 'What are you wearing?' he asked on the phone.

'A black leather jacket,' I said. 'But when I take it off I'll be in red and black. And what about you? Although I should be able to recognise you.' He'd told me that he was the only black man at the ballroom dance venues.

When I walked into the Grand Ballroom, it all looked pretty crowded, but I found a table towards the back where I would be able to see the dance floor and the rock and roll competition and watch the door.

He'd said on the phone that he'd be dressed in black and red too. So when an olive-skinned man in a maroon shirt and black trousers opened the door, I thought it might be Aravind. I gazed so intently he came over to the table.

'Is your name Aravind?' I asked.

'No,' he said. 'My name's Joe.'

'Oh! Sorry.'

He turned and walked over to the bar.

The place was pretty dark and I don't see very clearly at the best of times, let alone when I'm wearing those dreadful contact lenses.

'I don't know how you do it, Sofia,' Ingrid has said to me more than once. 'If anything happened to Dennis, I wouldn't be able to put myself out there like you do.'

Finally Aravind walked in. I knew it was him for sure and gave a wave. Even though I'd seen a photo of him on the dancing partner website, I was pleasantly surprised. Maybe it was the cut of the camel leather jacket he was wearing that padded out his shoulders, I don't know what it was – he hadn't mentioned a jacket. He was far more attractive than I expected.

He was looking around the place with a frown – two vertical lines between his eyebrows that cut his forehead into deep grooves. The Flaming Guitars were playing 'Blue Suede Shoes' up the front. The bar ran down one side opposite the door. I had already bought a lemon, lime and bitters – the standard choice for serious dancers. After all, I didn't want him to feel he needed to buy me a drink. He was out of work. Lost his job.

'Forget him,' snaps Ingrid as we walk along the path by the cliffs at Bondi and I tell her about my latest attempt to find a regular dance partner. I like her to know that I've got a life – that I'm not sitting at home in front of the television every night.

'Stay away,' she says emphatically. 'You don't want that. You don't want to start anything up with a man without a job.'

I ignore her and press on, determined to give her all the details. 'He walked over to my table. He looked so gorgeous. His thick black hair fell forward across his smooth dark skin. Sensitive eyes, generous mouth. I was really surprised.'

Ingrid slows down, almost stops.

'I couldn't think of a thing to say to him at first. He had this way of speaking, each word carefully chosen, English-school accent – I think boarding school in New Delhi. He took his jacket off, put his umbrella under the chair and dug his shiny, two-tone black and white dance shoes out of his bag. I sucked on my straw and tried not to stare at him.'

'I thought you'd seen a picture of him?' Ingrid says.

'Yes. Two photos on his website – password-protected, of course. He didn't look black to me, but I couldn't see him clearly. They weren't close ups. He said he and his wife call themselves "bar-b-cued ozzies".'

'Did his wife come and watch?'

'No.'

'Don't get involved with him. Don't break up a marriage,' Ingrid hisses, stumbling as the front of her runners catches on the path.

'You know I don't take any notice of things that you tell me,' I say, reaching out to steady her.

'Yes, but I'm sure you know better than to get involved with a married man.'

We walk on.

'His wife doesn't like to dance. He told me she encourages him to go out rather than sit at home looking miserable. I'd asked what she enjoys doing. He said she likes cooking, and that he loves eating her cooking. They used to have dance lessons together but she only did it to please him. He could tell from her body language that she didn't enjoy it. She won't even go to the club up the road with him.'

'His wife needs to watch out,' Ingrid says in a clipped voice that sounds just like her mother's. She gives me a gentle push on the shoulder to move me to the side of the track as two joggers pass.

'He said he keeps telling himself that it's important not to fall in love with his dance partner.'

Ingrid rolls her eyes and says, 'Oh, sure.'

'But the women you dance with know you're married with kids,' I'd said when he came back from the bar with his own glass of lemon, lime and bitters. He replied that you can't control that kind of thing. You can't control where your heart takes you. It just happens, he said. He has two dance partners already – one for competition and one for lessons. That's what the photos are on his website. Him and his two dance partners.'

'So why's he looking for another one?' Ingrid scoffs as she sips from her bottle of water.

'He doesn't go social dancing with the others. He doesn't like to have to do a particular sequence of steps all the time. He prefers to do whatever moves he feels like.'

'He's not very available with a wife and two dance partners,' Ingrid sniffs.

We walk on in silence.

'So, what happened then?' she asks with a sigh. 'You may as well tell me the whole story.'

'We got up for an old Elvis number, a slow rock and roll. That was the plan. We started with this style and then, depending how things worked out, we'd get on to the ballroom and the Latin at another time. We were going to have a few dances together and then watch the competition. But one of the men from the band came over to our table and asked us to enter the comp. He'd seen the two of us on the floor. He said that if we didn't put our names down, he wouldn't have enough people to make the competition worthwhile. "It's up to you," said Aravind. I told the man from the band that this was the first time Aravind and I had met, let alone danced. "Well, you look good together," he said. He wrote our names down on a piece of paper before going back to the stage.'

'So you danced with Aravind in the comp?' Ingrid asks grudgingly.

'What happened was he wanted to do some drops. He whispered it to me. "We can do some drops," his voice rising with excitement.'

'Drops? You didn't, did you? What about your back?'

'I know they're dangerous, especially with someone you've never danced with before and when you don't know their signals. I felt nervous but safe. Aravind is such a strong lead. I told him, though, that we'd have to go outside and practise on the footpath if we were going to do drops – except it was raining. He said I didn't have to do the drops if I didn't feel comfortable.'

Ingrid and I move aside to make room for a man with a collection of dogs on leads to pass us.

'Ingrid, I'd do anything just to keep on dancing with him – he's great. He's so much better than me. It's a real challenge. Apparently, I was beaming so much when we were dancing together that Simon said if I'd died right then and gone to heaven, I would have been happy. You know Simon? My old mate from years ago? He and his wife were there too. They entered the competition as well.'

'So, did you win?'

'We came second. Simon and his wife came third. They were a bit pissed off because they've been dancing together for years and it was our first time. We had to dance to two numbers, one fast and one slow. "Jail House Rock" and something else. I think it was "Wooden Heart". Anyway, we ended up coming second and winning a bottle of champagne – drops and all. And at the end, when they called out our names to come up and collect our prize, they said over the microphone that it was our first date and could be the beginning of something special.'

'So are you going to see him again?' Ingrid asks, her attention drawn to the ocean.

'He insisted that I take the bottle of champagne home and he carried it all the way to the car for me. The rain had stopped. He gave me a hug and a kiss on the cheek. It felt rather nice.'

'His wife really needs to watch out,' repeated Ingrid, leaning forward on the rail to get a better look at the rocks of Ben Buckler.

My mind wanders back to that night with Aravind.

After I drove home, I put the water on to boil for tea and had a shower. In the bathroom, I lifted my hair up off the back of my neck and smoothed my skin under the light and wondered when we'd dance together again. That night, I'd visited that very special place full of passion and excitement that I only ever touch through dance. I stared into the mirror, straightened up, belly pulled in, shoulders back, chest proud. I poured the water into the pot, selected a fine bone china mug from the cupboard and took the tray into the bedroom and hoped he'd ring soon.

'So here's the thing, Ingrid. I didn't know what to do next. I didn't know whether I should wait for him to initiate contact. Anyway, I was talking to my old mate Simon about it and he said that seeing how it's a dancing-only relationship – an equal arrangement – it's okay for me to ring Aravind. But Simon said not to wait too long if I wanted to dance with Aravind again. Not too long. Anyway, a few days later, Aravind emailed and invited me to partner him at a ball coming up in a couple of weeks. We ended up seated at the same table as his competition partner, Wilma. A tall, elegant blonde. "What are you doing here?" she asked me. "I invited Sofia," Aravind answered firmly on my behalf.'

'It's not looking so good,' Ingrid says as we head around the corner and down towards the café.

'Aravind had almost every dance with me at the ball, but when the opening bars of "Edelweiss" started up Wilma came over and invited him for a dance, saying to me, "It's our competition waltz."'

'Territorial,' Ingrid says in her I-told-you-so voice.

I won't go into it with Ingrid. I decide to change the subject. Today she's wearing her super-brief denim shorts, straw hat and big hoop earrings. She looks like an ageing hippy. She grips the rail that leads to the café like grim death as we descend the steps that bypass Waverley cemetery. Holding on to what, I wonder, as I gorge myself on spring's blossoming – the jacaranda in morning blue, bougainvillea in brilliant scarlet, the heady scent of jasmine.

Maybe Simon was right. Am I stuck in a rut, waiting?

And for what?

The Crystal Ballroom

Ingrid had been in the sea and was walking towards me wearing a loose-fitting, patterned dress, creamy white with a dark geometric pattern of triangles over her swimsuit. She'd tucked her dress in to her costume at the side, like the tennis players do, so it billowed open when she walked to reveal her bare, tanned, long and well-defined legs. She stopped to lean against the doorway at the café by the sea where I waited for her and lit up. She stood there one arm folded across her diaphragm and the elbow of the other resting on her forearm smoking her cigarette in that particular way of hers. Her fingers pushed two strands of limp blonde hair behind her ears. 'It's good for you to dance,' she said. 'Just treat it like a job. You just have to go. That's what I'd do.'

'Yes. I wish I was as self-disciplined as you, to just be able to do the things that I know are good for me.'

'What's the point in sitting at home? It's no answer.'

'There is no answer.'

Just dance one night a week to begin with, Ingrid counselled. Don't overdo it. And don't expect too much. Just go for the dancing. Well, of course I said that that was all I go for. She warned me not to get caught up in all the other stuff.

The next time I saw Aravind was when he invited me to partner him at the Christmas dance. I'd arrived early – far too early. I handed over the entry fee to the two women who sat at a table at the door and waited there for Aravind.

'Who are you waiting for?' they asked.

'Aravind,' I said. 'You know him, I'm sure.'

They nodded.

'He's really nice,' I said. 'But I know he's taken.'

'It's impolite to keep a lady waiting,' said Krista, pressing her lips together.

They do seem nice, Beverley and Krista. Beverley likes to dress up in clown-like clothes and make everyone laugh. Like after they played that silly but funny game of being the first person to rush to the stage with your dance partner's belt or shoe, or whatever item was announced each time the music stopped. At the end, when the game was finished, Beverley was shoving or dangling from her hand, or waving about, or whatever she was doing to attract people's attention, a pair of black and red lace knickers. And then she put them on, on top of her shiny green shorts.

People were dressed in the Christmas colours of red and green, although most of the dancers chose red and black, the women in dresses pinched at the waist and the men in black trousers and open-neck shirts. One of the women was in a sparkling lamé number, a tight shift to just above her knees. Not the best choice for ballroom dancing.

That night after supper, when two tables at the end of the sprung wooden dance floor were laden with dainty sandwiches, squares of fruit cake and platters of watermelon and cherries, when people had returned to their tables on the edge of the dance floor, when the ballroom dancing had come to an end, Krista was up the front leading a macarena. She was hamming it up, doing pelvic thrusts each time the dancers had to turn in another direction. She wore an even brighter outfit than usual and, buttoned tight into her bodice, the upper part of her body was so stiff and motionless that it seemed as if all the life in her had descended to her hips. They gyrated round and round and back and forth as she flitted around the room, her deep pockets full of lollies to be handed out as a lucky dip. You had to dig your hand deep into her skirt to get one.

Anyway, it was Krista who was watching Aravind and me at the dance, she who saw Aravind's competition partner Wilma come up and say to Aravind, 'Why aren't you two dancing? Every time I look at you both, you're just sitting there.'

He became defensive at once when Wilma came over to our table. He told her that neither of us were crazy about the New Vogue brackets, but then he went off and asked some other woman to dance. He was doing his good Samaritan thing and inviting someone who had been sitting out. But if that Wilma hadn't said anything, he would have stayed chatting with me. He'd said previously that he wanted to have conversations with his new dance partner rather than dance every dance.

I don't know why Wilma invited that fellow Paul to partner her at the Christmas dance. He's one of the regulars. Wilma is the one with the legs to her armpits. The one Ingrid refers to as The Bitch. Tall willowy Wilma. Ingrid likes to describe me as short and stocky, but other people tell me I'm petite. That Wilma acts like she owns Aravind. I know he's her comp partner.

'Sofia,' Paul said to me, 'apparently Wilma asked Aravind did he mind if she invited someone else to the Christmas dance and he said that was fine. He told her he'd have no problem finding another partner.'

So Aravind asked me.

I don't get it. Isn't Aravind a good enough dancer for her? I admit he is very difficult to follow at times. He said he's sick of having to keep to a particular sequence of steps, like he and Wilma learn at their private lessons. He prefers to ad lib.

'Do you want to swap partners?' Wilma commanded when she came up to our table and invited Aravind up for a waltz.

'How do you feel about being swapped?' I said to Paul.

'Partner swap? That reminds me of the sixties,' he laughed.

Paul and I began to dance to a slow waltz. The room seemed to rise and fall with each sliding step. It was as if we were figure skating. I held my breath, not wanting to lose concentration when the music increased in speed and we were waltzing to music that seemed as fast as a jitterbug. As we swung past the doors, I saw Wilma's green dress blow up past her knees, her legs intertwined with Aravind's. They looked good together in their matching Christmas green, although I was trying hard not to watch her. Her head thrown back, her throat exposed. Aravind's spine was arched, his arms rigid, his chin pulled in, his chest up and forward. Paul was waltzing me along, stepping it out with long strides faster than ever. We turned, and everything around us revolved – chandeliers, leaded glass, mirrors, the velvet and brocade furnishings.

At the end of the dance, Aravind walked me to my car. We stood there, the driver's door open, as the others gradually left the building. They got into their cars behind us.

A gentle breeze blew across the back of my neck as he moved in towards me. A bird called out in the cool night air. We'd been so hot in the ballroom, even though there was air conditioning. The heat, the sweat, the feel of his green silk shirt under my hand.

It felt good to be finally outside in the crisp night, my hair wet at the back making the breeze even sharper. The sound of car doors shutting, the street light highlighting the ferns on the perimeter of the road. Even in the midnight shadows, you could see the green of their fronds and the brown of their trunks.

The wind audible above the goodbyes from the dance hall, the door open behind us. Krista and her band of helpers were packing up the tables and chairs. Aravind was planning to go back in and help with the cleaning up. Krista had asked him to come in the afternoon to help set up the room but he was busy at home and offered to help clean up at the end instead. Wilma, no doubt, was inside helping. At least she wasn't outside standing over us while we said our goodbyes.

Aravind had his arms around me. The smooth texture of his silk shirt under my hands again. I couldn't smell any body odour even though he said he'd been sweating. I didn't let the hug go on for too long, though. After all, he's married.

The time before, I'd parked in a side street and at the end of the dance I'd asked him to drive me to my car. His car was parked on the gravel inside a parking area. It was a low-slung immaculately presented navy blue model with cream leather seats and a big polished mahogany steering wheel. Not a book or piece of paper thrown anywhere, not like in my car.

That was the night when I got to sit beside him in his car, to sit in the space where his wife would be, and saw the spotless interior and the dark blue of his BMW. Not that I'm into cars.

That first time at that first dance when we'd won the bottle of champagne in the rock and roll competition, he'd said that it was a shame we live so far apart. 'This might sound funny,' he said, 'and I know you're not a child, but I'd like you to give me a call or send me a text when you get home – just to let me know you've arrived safely.' He really is so good looking. 'I'll come over your way next time," he said. 'I'll come and pick you up.'

Ingrid lifts her hand that holds the cigarette and shades her eyes against the late-afternoon glare. Waiters are setting the now empty tables with white table cloths, silver cutlery and wine glasses, ready for the early dinner crowd. Out on the bay a white sail passes in front of a green and yellow ferry heading towards Circular Quay and for a moment there is only the sound of the waves unfurling on the sand. Then the breeze drops and the sail disappears around the headland.

Ingrid drags deeply on her cigarette and her mouth relaxes into a grimace for a fraction of a second. 'What do you want from him? If he comes to your place?'

'He's very attractive.'

'Attractive?'

'Handsome.'

Tom

May Ling steps across the skipping rope. I'm waiting for her with her baby brother, outside the school hall, but she hasn't seen me yet. Every Thursday when she finishes her hip hop class, I hang about with the other mothers and grandmothers and carers. It's a routine I enjoy – walking up here with the baby in the stroller and then chatting with May Ling as we walk home.

May Ling is my son's daughter. She has straight black hair and brown almond eyes, slim legs and tiny hands. Her hands are artistic: she draws beautiful pictures. In her black strappy shoes and blue-and-white school dress that falls below her knees, she looks very grown-up.

The park is on the bend of the road that leads to the school. There is a sandpit, swings, slippery dip, climbing chains and a rocking horse. We put our things down on one of the wooden benches on the perimeter of the park and sit in the shade of the trees. I unpack the afternoon tea: three apples, two bottles of water, rice crackers, sultana biscuits, peanut butter sandwiches.

The other mothers and carers come over and start up a conversation. What beautiful children. How old are they? What nationality?

'Their mother is Chinese,' I explain.

Some women are envious; they wish their own mothers would mind the children when they go to work or play golf.

I've got the bucket and spades and the plastic rakes hanging off one of the handles of the stroller ready for the sandpit. I keep them in the boot of the car between visits. Also in the boot is the collapsible stroller, the picnic blanket, the extra booster seat, the beach chair and the Cancer Council tent all folded up tight in its blue bag. I'm prepared for all possibilities.

When we leave the park, we stop outside the rose garden of the RSL club so May Ling can pick a flower to take home to her mummy. Sometimes we sing a song from *The Wizard of Oz*. Today May Ling is chanting, Where's my daddy? Where's my daddy? I'd said to her that he might drive past and give her a lift like he'd done once before.

Ingrid said she's surprised that with all his qualifications he can't get a job. I said he doesn't want *any* job. It has to be the *right* job, even if it takes him six months – yet again – to find it.

Last week I was standing in the kitchen at his house and he was rinsing the plates on the bench and stacking them into the dishwasher. I told him that May Ling had asked if Mummy and Daddy were getting a divorce. He laughed and said he would have to tell her to stop telling me things.

'Don't stop her from talking to me,' I said. 'Everyone fights. I told her that.'

After dinner and when it's time for him to go upstairs to run a bath, I say my goodbyes. I am not allowed to go up because they all get in the bath together. He gives me a couple of chocolates from out of the fridge to eat on my way home before kissing me on the cheek at the front door.

'Drive carefully, Sofia,' he calls out as I head towards the car.

When I'd told him about the split-up with Tom, he'd said he could never understand what on earth I'd seen in the man.

A counsellor had told me that a lot of people continue in a relationship because they don't want to go through the pain of breaking up. 'In six months' time, you won't feel a thing,' he said in an effort to reassure me.

I shrugged. 'The grandchildren won't be pleased.'

'Grandma's broken up with her surfie boyfriend,' he joked.

A seagull, wings flapping calmly and evenly, passes this place where I sit. It's a crescent-shaped bay on the harbour where a man and a woman walk hand in hand along the beach, their dog running ahead. Tiny ripples on the water drift gently towards the shore.

Tom seemed calm at first, after I said what must have disappointed him, but then he became withdrawn and went into the bathroom. He cleaned his teeth and then came back out. He pulled the sheets back on the bed. He got in and appeared to fall asleep straight away.

'Goodnight,' I said to his back.

'I thought I said goodnight,' he said, turning towards me.

'Goodnight,' I said kissing him on the cheek.

He turned away again.

I can see now that Tom felt out of his depth at my younger son's wedding and I feel remorse for hurting him.

Ingrid had counselled, 'His mother probably said to him, "I told you she'd drop you after the wedding."'

A row of tall dark cypress trees shield the beach from the road. On one of the wooden bench chairs by the water sits a woman dressed all in black.

'What's your mother like?' I asked him.

'She sits in a corner and does what she's told,' he said. 'I sat up with her last night and we watched a movie. What do you think of that?'

'I think it's dreadful – dreadful that you're still living there with your parents.'

'It's very difficult for me. Very difficult. It's the money.'

'What do you want from him?' his mother said to me, unable to hide the hatred in her voice, when I'd called that one time.

I told Tom what his mother said.

He wanted to say to her, 'Are you pleased – are you pleased now? Have you got what you want?'

So now I am back to how things had been before, alone at nights, and as though he had never existed.

In the school holidays, May Ling usually stays for a day or two at my place. One day recently, she came running up the steps carrying a drawing and a poster of a horse. I came out to meet her, wiping my hands on the chequered tea towel. I'm sure my face was flushed from the heat. May Ling's floral skirt was almost to her ankles as she kicked off her shoes at the back door. I said to her that she looked as pretty as a picture.

'Do you have the photos? The ones of Daddy when he was a baby? I've been waiting all day to see the photos.'

'Yes, yes. Come on in and we'll get out the album.'

The last of the sun's light slanted through the blinds as we sat side by side turning the pages.

'You don't look anything like you used to look,' she said.

'It was a long time ago,' I sighed. 'My hair's not the same. Poppy looks very different too, don't you think?'

She shook her head. 'No. He looks the same to me. Poppy looks the same.'

'It must be my hairstyle.'

'Why did you and Poppy divorce?'

'I got married too young. I was only a teenager.'

'Did you have a fight?'

I didn't answer, so she moved the conversation on to the split up with Tom. She's let me know several times that she's upset about it and can't understand why it's happened.

'And what about you and Tom and your divorce?' she asked, rolling her eyes upward. 'Or whatever you call it. The divorce that isn't a divorce. Did you have a fight?'

'Yes, I told you before.'

'What about?'

'It was about a couple of things.'

'What did you fight about?'

'I told you one of the things.'

'I've forgotten. What things?'

'It's very hard to tell you because you're only six years old and you mightn't understand.'

'Tell me and I'll tell you if I understand.'

'Well, it's hard to say exactly. Like, can you put into words why you didn't like that teacher at school, except that she expected too much of you?'

'Yes. She asked us to draw our favourite place. I said, Port Stephens is my favourite place but I don't know how to draw it. She said, Just do it, and didn't give me any help. Miss McDonald used to help us do things. Not, Do this, do that. So there, I've said it. It's your turn now.'

I was uncomfortable having this conversation with May Ling. Her father has warned me that she will persist and persist and persist until she gets the answers and the more you try to escape her questions the more she persists. May Ling is not like other six-year-olds. Her parents treat her as an equal and she appears to be very mature. She knows I met Tom at a dance. It was a 'meet your match' dance and you had to choose a name for yourself from the name cards laid out at the front door when you arrived. Like Batman and Robin, Bec and Lleyton. You chose a card and had to find your matching partner. He selected Tarzan and I chose Jane.

'Well, I told you the bit about the photo,' I said.

'What photo?'

'When I saw the photo in his wallet. It was a rude picture.'

'A bare bottom?'

'No, the top half.'

'Of a friend?'

'No. He cut the photo out of a magazine.'

'Who was she?'

'No one he knew. Just someone he'd cut out of a magazine. There was no photo of his sons or of me.'

'I don't think that's so bad,' she said. 'What else happened? You said there were two things?'

'He was a lot younger.'

'You could have said your birthday came before his.'

'Well, what do you think would be a good reason?'

'If he found another girlfriend.'

Outside, a van rounded the bend of the road and disappeared down the hill with a swooshing sound.

After a pause, I said, 'I remember now why we split up. The problem was that I didn't love him and he said he loved me.'

She frowned. 'Well, let's play a game. One of us is Tom and the other one is you and we have the fight.'

'No, darling. Let's go upstairs and have a story. It's late. It's already past your bedtime.'

'Let's do it, Sofia. I'll be Tom.' She scowled at me, her brows knitted in a triangle. 'Oh, Sofia,' she pleaded.

'If you go to bed now, I'll let you choose the story or otherwise I'll chose it.'

She crossed her arms with a 'Humph.' Then, 'Well, show me how you used to dance with Tom. You said that's where you met him.

Taking her hand, I said, 'Come on, darling.'

We went up to her bedroom and she looked through her bookcase carefully for the appropriate story. No Dr Seuss or *The Little Mermaid* tonight. Instead she decided on *Beauty and the Beast*: the story of a man who is unable to love someone, so he's turned into an ugly beast.

It was dark in the lounge room, but I didn't open the shutters. I didn't feel anything in particular; no hate, no repugnance. I had agreed that he could come when he asked the previous evening. I paid close attention to the sounds, to the light, to the noises in the park next door that had enveloped the room. He looked at me stretched out on the couch expecting me to speak. I didn't look him in the face. Didn't look at him at all.

'You'll see,' he said. 'It will be better this time. Things will be better.' He removed my shoes, threw them on the floor. 'So you'll give me another chance?' He knelt beside me. Didn't say any more that he loves me. Said, 'It's a comfort to know we'll keep seeing each other.'

I didn't answer.

'That's all I want,' he said. 'Just to know I'm going to see you.' He unzipped my jeans.

'You know it will end again,' I said.

'Not too soon, though. Will it?'

Slowly. Slow, patient. With my eyes shut. 'I don't know.'

'I'm prepared to take the risk,' he said. 'I want to. I don't want to not see you again.'

I stroked his hair.

He pulled off his T-shirt. Undressed himself.

A seagull, wings flapping gently and evenly, passes this place where I sit. He skirts the line of the beach between water and sand and finally comes to rest on the top rung of the railing that defines the path to the beach.

'Sex is good for you,' the female doctor had said, moving back to her desk.

It was a routine examination.

'Us women need the testosterone,' she added with a little smile.

I'd wanted to end it again, it must have been for the fifth time. After the phone call, I felt angry and wanted to tell him not to come. I was letting him visit against my will, since I was still angry. The next night and for several nights after that I wanted to tell him not to come. He'd conducted himself in a way that disgusted me. He denied he'd had a couple of drinks and said he was tired, that no, he hadn't been drinking, he was just tired.

I was silent at first, after he said what repulsed me, but then he sensed my lack of warmth and said he'd call again before the weekend. He asked who I was going out to dinner with and I said it was a married couple, some friends who had invited other friends of mine. I didn't want to include him in the invitation because he'd feel uncomfortable with these people and this would make me ill at ease too. He could come on the Friday.

'You were waiting for him to grow up, but he hasn't,' the counsellor had said forcefully, with intention, as was his way. 'It won't work. You'll get bored with him again. You don't like the uncertainty. You're in control in this relationship. You're the adult. He's the child. It's your call – your choice. I just try to give you support.'

The wind blows from the south. The waves soften at their edges. May Ling is playing in the sand with her red bucket. She's looking for schools of fish to catch, the white plastic ice cream container full of shells and sand and seaweed. Her small fingers rearrange the pieces of her collection. A seaplane labours against the wind, not quite balanced between sea and clouds.

'May Ling,' I call out. 'Look at the seaplane.'

She looks up through the brim of her black eyelashes then walks up towards me. 'Look what I've got,' she says, opening her fingers.

'What, sugar plum?'

'Shells.'

'Have you ever collected shells before?'

'No.' She puts them into the plastic container filled with seawater and sand. 'A fish tank,' she says proudly.

'Do you like this beach?'

She shrugs. 'It's not too bad.'

She walks back to the water's edge, tiptoeing between the rocks and the flotsam and jetsam that the waves have left on the shore, skipping across the moss-covered stones.

'Sofia, can you come in with me?' she calls out. 'Come into the water and help me catch some fish.'

There is the sound of the waves lapping the shore. Butterflies – mostly turquoise and black – more colour than the birds, flit between the branches and flap in front of the harbour. The seaplane finishes its circling and lands not far from the beach.

'There's something so wonderful about watching the waves,' Tom had said. 'Especially when you've just been out there, and come back in. Afterwards I always like to just sit on the sand and watch the waves.'

May Ling comes back up to where I sit under a tree on the grass. 'I'm hungry,' she says. 'Did you bring anything to eat?'

I reach for the cooler bag and unzip it. 'What would you like?'

May Ling looks in at the food and frowns. 'Is that all?'

She reaches for a small carton of apple juice and sips quickly on the straw before handing it back.

'Isn't it any good?'

She smirks. 'It tastes off.' She turns around and walks back towards the sea.

'It tastes fine to me,' I call out.

She yells from the water's edge, 'Sof, can you come in?'

The water is all green and slippery shimmering in the sunlight.

Yesterday I had lunch at a Japanese restaurant after a visit to the gym. It was not unusual for me to be there at that time, no more unusual than all the other people sitting alone on bar stools as the small containers of food did their revolutions. Jason, a friend I hadn't seen for a long time, was manipulating his chopsticks with great intensity. He was greying, confident, but struggling to attract patients to his new psychology practice.

'They can see value in spending money on a massage,' he complained, 'but not in a visit to someone like me.'

After we talked about our work and our families and our lives in general under the glare of the fluorescent light, he raised his eyebrows and gave his opinion on the relationship with Tom 'I have to be honest. I feel very angry. If it was a man in the same situation, people would say, dirty old man. But for a woman it's okay. Someone that age has a prick that's ready morning, noon and night. I'm more interested in a mature woman – someone I can really talk to. I'm not interested in young women. They might have great bodies but that doesn't do it for me.'

'What do you think, Sofia? Do they look okay? Is this what you'd imagined I'd wear to the beach – Sofia? Do I look all right? Is this what you'd imagined me wearing when you said we'd go for a swim this weekend?'

'I hadn't imagined you on the beach,' my irritated voice had answered from the bed. 'I hadn't thought about what you'd be wearing on the beach.'

He'd been preening himself from side to side in front of the mirror opposite the sun-drenched rosy pink chaise longue – pale against the warm tones; but when he walked back towards the mirror, he turned bronze again from head to foot, in his shiny black swimmers. His fine body hair covered his legs and arms.

'Usually I don't wear a costume under my wetsuit,' he said, 'so I bought these Speedos and a pair of board shorts. Which ones do you think I should wear to the beach?'

'You can wear both. Wear the Speedos under the board shorts.'

He was standing in front of the sliding mirrored doors that framed the wardrobe opposite two windows, looking at the reflection of a very boyish, very attractive figure, not very tall or very small, with blond loose curly hair like that of a cherub. He pulled on the cord of his swimming costume, puffed out his hard freckled chest, curved like a suit of armour. The whites of his hazel eyes and his white regular teeth glowed through the apricot warmth of the room.

'It's fine, Tom,' I reassured him. 'They look fine. You haven't got any white marks from the wetsuit. Either costume looks fine. Whatever you feel comfortable in. You can wear whatever you want.'

He grinned. 'I've never owned a pair of Speedos. I've watched blokes on the beach in their Speedos walking up from the water.'

'It's fine.'

He laughed to himself, unable to disguise the pride in his voice. 'They call these swimming costumes budgie smugglers. That's what they're called now.'

'Ingrid's eyes will pop out of her head when she sees you at Nielson Park today.'

Tom, motionless in front of his own image, laughed again to himself. 'I know so well not to wear the wrong thing when I'm with you.'

'I thought you were using your head instead of...' Ingrid said, unable to hold back the intensity of her disapproval. She had been showing me the latest photos of her new dog. She is very happy with Skippy and has said that he is good company and that he sleeps on her bed.

Before telling her I was back with Tom again, I'd said I had something to say, but please don't pass judgement. She spat the words at me.

'It's not that,' I said. 'That's not the motivation. It's for the companionship.'

'Companionship? You can have that with girlfriends. Tom has no conversation.'

'But he's easy to be with. It's nice to go out for a meal or to the movies.'

'Movies are good. You don't talk and there's something going on.' She sipped her latte then added, 'He's not the answer.'

'There is no answer. It's the loneliness. I can't stand the loneliness.'

She nodded then sat more upright in her chair. 'We're all different. It's a long way for him to travel, though.'

'Three hours either way.'

'Must be worth his while.'

'It might last a week, a month, a year, who knows. If you get the big C diagnosis, you could be dead in a few weeks.'

She shrugged. 'We all make our decisions. That's why I bought my little Skippy.' She put his puppy photos back into her handbag.

The ocean must be calm today. No energetic crashing coming from the direction of the sea. This morning I'm inside protected from the heat behind heavy curtains. I can't see the water.

'Messenger boy,' he'd laughed, referring to himself, on an overcast Saturday morning, after he's brought me a cup of tea in bed and was about to go up the road to buy the newspaper.

'Having you just completes my life,' he said when he finished reading the sports pages. 'I can't think of anything nicer than sitting on the bed with you on a morning like this. After the weekend, I'm going to go back feeling so good. Thank you so much.'

He stretched himself out on the chaise longue that was under the window next to the bed and said, 'Everyone's got someone. Why shouldn't we? Who cares what anyone else thinks? It's between you and me.'

'What did your parents say when you said you were coming to Sydney this weekend?'

He grinned. 'Nothing. When I said goodbye, Dad said to Mum, Just let him go.'

'Did your mother say something?'

'No.'

'How do you feel about your parents going away for two months on Monday?'

'Okay.'

'Last time you were worried before they went away. But you know now how to use the washing machine.'

'I've got it all written down. I've got it written in a book.'

'What's the resolution of the story?' May Ling asks, sprinkling grated cheese on her pasta.

'How do you know these things?' I say. 'Who tells you?'

'At school.'

'In first class at school they teach you about the resolution of a story?'

'In the library. What's the problem that starts the story?'

'Do you know what resolution means?

'It means how things turn out in the end.'

I look to my son and daughter-in-law. 'What will they teach them in Year Twelve if they learn this in first class already?'

'You haven't answered me,' interrupts May Ling. 'I'm listening,' she says with a hand to her ear.

'It's very hard for me to explain these things to you,' I say yet again.

'What are the complexities of the story?' she asks.

I turn to my son for help.

'The story's about a woman who's looking for love,' he says to his daughter.

'There are many kinds of love,' I apologise. 'Not just between a man and a woman. Love for children…grandchildren.'

A quiet still morning. Water trickles down through the rocks after last night's rain. Several different bird calls in the gully. Intermittent hammering in the unit above. The large heavy curtains barely parted to keep out the eastern heat, but open enough to see the leaves of a tree rustling in the morning sea breeze that blows across my feet.

Tom and I had stood at the window and looked through the bare branches and realised that now we could see all the way to the horizon at Bondi. The ridge blocked the line of the horizon but we could see the clouds that hung just above it. We'd loved watching the sky.

'I've seen the sky looking like this before,' he'd said, putting his arm around my waist.

'What do you mean?'

'So still. A winter sky.'

At the back door before he left, he said, 'So you think there's still heat in the furnace?'

I'd laughed and nodded.

'That's what the expression is, isn't it?'

'I don't know. I haven't heard it. Heat in the fire? It probably feels like a furnace to you.'

'It works well being casual like this,' he said. 'We don't have to deal with each other's problems.'

I asked Ingrid what she thought he meant by that. She said it was probably something he'd heard someone else say.

'I've been thinking about it – wondering what he meant.'

'Nothing,' she said. 'He didn't mean anything. He just says things that he hears other people say.'

'I'm very proud to be seen with you,' he'd said. 'A younger man with an older woman. I'm not ashamed to be seen with you.'

Now, I sit by the water until the sun goes down. Then walk back home.

Martin

It's the Easter long weekend and Martin's chest is pressed up against mine in a tango. We are dancing on a wooden floor under a marquee at the Easter Music and Dance Festival. Rain drips off the edges of the canvas on to the chairs that surround the square teak floor. Martin's woollen jacket is very heat-making, too hot to have jammed up against me. A couple of rounds of the floor, moving in sync to the complex rhythms and elusive melodies of the six violins, and we are perspiring.

He is tall, around my age, with finely etched features, hair turning grey at the edges, eyes as turquoise as the Mediterranean. They entice you like cooling waves on a hot and humid day.

He looks good in his black trousers, white shirt and black wool blazer. I'm wearing the same old safe black pants and a red voile embroidered top. Martin chose what he'd wear for this evening of dance before we met up for a takeaway at the campsite. He dressed in a fashion that meant he had a bet either way – he could meet up with that woman who invited him to partner her at the Farewell Ball, or he could dance tango under the tarpaulin with me.

Earlier, I stood in a queue for two Moroccan lamb with couscous while he went off to buy a bottle of wine. He put ten dollars in my hand and went in search of one of the on-site bars to buy a red.

I am very pleased we bumped into each other at the New Vogue workshop on the first day of the festival. My friend Amanda is hardly available. I never know where she is and have given up trying to meet up with her since she dropped me off at the motel. Amanda has hired one of the Tent City pre-erected on-site tents not too far from the session bar. She hangs out at that place until late every night.

'That's where people go when everywhere else has closed down,' Martin said.

Amanda refers to him as 'your Martin'. He's not mine of course – although I really like him. He's just someone I met years ago at the Crystal Ballroom and haven't seen since. He was an outrageous flirt on the floor, especially in the rumba – the dance of love. That side of my life has been pretty quiet ever since. A long time between drinks, to coin a cliché – although I know that the way you look at these things is all relative.

Each day of the five-day festival, Martin and I have met up for a meal or a dance – usually by chance. We turn up at the same workshops or are part of the same crowd eating porridge at the poets breakfast or we see each other standing in line for a chai latte or a piece of meat cooked over an open fire, there among the food and craft stalls that line the streets near the performance areas. Thousands of people, hundreds of musicians. He comes every year, apparently, usually with his girlfriend. He told me they broke up recently. She kept saying that she loved him, but he doesn't feel the same way about her.

'It gets very cold in my tent without her, though,' he sighs as the palm of his hand presses firmly into my back guiding me around the congested floor as the passion of a Piazolla number encompasses the marquee.

I open my eyes and look up at him. 'Missing your hot water bottle?'

He laughs as he manoeuvres between the couples in the close embrace of the dance. Some women with their heads resting against the man's shoulder, others cheek to cheek, the women's arm raised and behind the neck of the man in an intimate embrace. All dressed in the traditional costume of tango – black trousers, red shirts, red dresses.

'You wouldn't have any trouble finding a new girlfriend. You must meet lots of women at the dances.'

'The problem is that after a while the well runs dry. You've drained the well.'

I close my eyes again in order to relax into the pleasure of the dance, to concentrate properly on the complicated rhythms of Piazolla's music, to feel and interpret Martin's lead, to respond to his intentions that are signalled by the position of his chest against mine.

Later in the evening, after the intensity and drama of the tango has ended, he suggests we go for a drink. 'If you're prepared to stay up later tonight?'

'It's just that I don't want to miss the last bus.'

He changes out of his dance shoes and I put on my coat and scarf and we walk across the pathway to the session bar. It's packed with men and women with pink cheeks and down jackets and chequered flannel shirts. A jam session is happening in one of the corners. I offer to buy him a drink and line up to get a coupon. The ticket seller seems a bit drunk, but he's very friendly and welcoming. It's nice. In fact, I stand there with the drinks waiting for Martin to appear again and keep a smile on my face for the rest of the evening, and when we meet up again back in Sydney a few weeks later. It's the Crystal Ballroom's ten-year anniversary concert and I'm still smiling.

He told me at the Music and Dance Festival that he'd be coming along to the anniversary concert and I arrived early with Ingrid. I keep a smile on my face when Martin comes and sits with us, even though it's only because there isn't a spare chair anywhere else in the room. He puts his jacket on the seat next to mine and places his shoe bag under the table. I keep that smile plastered on my face even when he goes off for the whole night to dance with the blonde with the hair to her waist and I leave.

At the session bar at the Music and Dance Festival, Martin and I drink our beers quickly, because it's very noisy and crowded and we can't hear ourselves speak, and because I'm worrying about how to get back to my motel if I miss the bus. We walk out of the bar and head out into the freezing night air. It is midnight. He says he can give me a lift if I don't mind the long trek to his car. He's camping on the outskirts of the showground. I thought my motel would be within walking distance of the festival, but it turned out to be a fairly long slog.

We stroll around the perimeter of the grounds toward the exit gates. He's talking all the time, telling me about when he used to go on camping holidays as a child with his father. He tells me he brings an ice cream bucket to urinate in at night. But when he was here with his girlfriend he had to bring a bigger one. I try to imagine a woman squatting over an ice cream container peeing in a tent.

Ingrid laughs when I tell her this bit. We are having a drink waiting for the band to set up at the Crystal Ballroom's ten-year anniversary concert. It's a couple of weeks since the Music and Dance Festival. At the other end of the room, the band is assembling and we watch as they extract their trumpets from their cases.

Ingrid asks if Edward, one of the regulars, was at the festival too. 'You know Edward? Very tall Edward. The one who likes nothing better than a cup of tea and a good chat.'

'Yes, yes. He was there on a day visit. He had all the goss on Martin.'

'He's like a girlfriend the way you can talk to him about anything. He's got all the info on everyone. Or he thinks he does.'

'Yes, he said he'd seen Martin dance with the old girlfriend at other venues and according to him she's young and beautiful and a great dancer. But Martin didn't want to be tied down and answerable to her jealous accusations. Edward said they looked fantastic on the dance floor. Very sexy.'

'He's good like that.'

'Anyway, Martin was sort of making a line for me, I think, and one night when I'd missed the last bus back to my motel at the festival he offered to give me a lift. No problems at the door to my room – I didn't ask him in and he didn't make any moves. We hadn't exchanged telephone numbers – I didn't want to be the first one to ask.'

In front of Ingrid and me, other members of the band arrive and unpack their instruments. Eventually the discordant sound of the twenty-one-piece big band tuning up engulfs the ballroom. It's really hard to get a table at the Crystal Ballroom these days. As soon as the raffle ends, you have to pounce.

'So Amanda invited you to the Music and Dance Festival but didn't spend any time with you?' Ingrid shouts above the noise. 'That's not much of a friend.'

'She didn't invite me. She offered to give me a lift. She's your friend anyway, not mine.'

Ingrid shrugs and sips her brandy lime and soda.

'I think Amanda was jealous of my friendship with Martin. He's good-looking, well dressed, seems intelligent enough and is an accomplished dancer. When Amanda met that guy, Chris, she referred to him as her version of my Martin.'

The lights dim as the band begins to play 'Second Hand Rose'.

'I wish they wouldn't turn the lights down so low,' Ingrid moans. 'You can't see a thing. You can't see when someone across the room is giving you the nod asking for a dance.'

It is a cold winter's night and I'm lying in bed under the doona listening to the hum of traffic on the main road outside. There isn't much noise at this time of night, just the occasional car. A plane overhead. The sighing of the heater.

I'm remembering when I stood up to leave the Crystal Ballroom at the ten-year anniversary and looked down at Martin's jacket draped on the back of the chair, his shoe bag still under the table. A horrible emptiness settled over me as the chandeliers shone crazily over the empty seat until it was too humiliating to bear and I had to turn away.

Amanda had told me that Martin went back to the session bar that night after he'd dropped me off at my motel. I didn't want to hear the details. She couldn't wipe the grin off her face as she spoke.

Now I'm listening to the gaps between the noise of the cars. The silence between the sounds that gets longer as the evening deepens and the long night moves slowly towards the dawn.

Keirin

You run up the stairs to the gym avoiding the women and men from the previous class rushing down the stairs. Keep to the left. Give your membership card to the girl at the desk and then in through the turnstile. Rummage for the two-dollar coin in your bag that works the locker. Insert the money, leave the bag, take the towel and the bottle of water and the book to read then up the stairs to the third floor to the exercise bikes all the time hoping there'll be a reclining bicycle free and not one of those awful uprights that hurt your bum. Sit on the bike, read your book, wipe the sweat off your face, drink from the bottle, look out the window to the workers erecting a block of apartments that are gradually blocking the view of the harbour. Warm up for sixty seconds on a low speed, then twenty minutes at a higher speed and a sixty-second cool down. Then into the main gym for the body power class. Get a step, four platforms, a rubber mat and a long weights bar. Two large discs, four small discs. Stand up the front so you can see yourself in the mirror and in front of the fan. Fight for this prime position. First the warm up, then legs, lunges, squats, chest, back, shoulders, legs, triceps, biceps, stomach. Bend from the hips. Clean and press. Dead rows. Wipe the sweat from your face, adjust the bar across your shoulders. Knees over toes as you squat. Straight back, stomach in to support the back, shoulders back, head up out of the neck. Concentrate on the music, the instructor speaking, the fan in front of you. Watch yourself in the mirror, the women beside you and behind. Check out how old they are and if their weights are heavier or lighter. Smell the sweat. Swallow the water. A quick stretch between tracks. Calves, quads, shoulders and back. Lie down on the platform for the chest track. Use your nipples as markers. Down to the markers, up slowly. One, two, three up and then slowly down. Vary the rhythm.

The telephone rang while she was running the bath. She stood in front of the mirror examining the droops of fat below her shoulder blades, the second fold at her waist. She turned around further noticing the dimpled flesh in a widening rear. She stopped and listened and then turned off the bath. She went to answer the telephone.

Hello.

Sofia, he said. How are you? What are you doing tonight?

Hi, Dennis. Nothing.

Well, come over for dinner. We've invited a friend, a single bloke, and we thought maybe you'd like to come too. He told me to tell you he's coming.

Who?

Keirin. He's split up with his wife in Port Macquarie and lives with his mother in Bondi.

Not that older bloke, the dentist you introduced me to ages ago?

No, not him. This is Keirin.

Not that doctor with the practice on Bondi Road who lives with his mother?

No. Not him. Don't worry about it. It's only a dinner.

Sofia could hear Dennis relaying the conversation to Ingrid in the background on the other end of the phone. Sofia looked out of the window to the huge spears of bamboo projecting from the floor of gully like giant asparagus shoots and wondered when the man was coming to cut it back. She remembered meeting Dennis at uni, so many years ago now. They'd met in a yoga class and then bumped into each other in Vietnam and she'd travelled around with him on the back of his motorbike. When he got back from Vietnam, Ingrid, his girlfriend, had moved in with him. The three of them had been friends ever since.

What time do you want me to come over? Sofia said.

Seven. And bring your photos.

It's been a long time since I've been with a bloke, she said to Dennis, her voice dropping lower. A bloody long time.

You don't want it to close over now, do you?

She laughed. That was Dennis, always going on about sex. Tantric sex was his speciality. So he said.

Sofia reversed up the driveway backing into the turning circle beside the rubbish bins. Up the driveway and out on to the street. As she drove, she looked at the people who hurried along the sidewalks arm in arm. She glanced at the darkening sky, filled with clouds, and at the houses with high fences and flowers in the front. She was feeling pretty dreadful, as she usually did at weekends. No one seemed to understand but she just didn't fit in any more. The children grown up and left, the business finished, the house gone. She looked out on to the street to remind herself there was a world out there.

She parked outside the block of units at Clovelly and turned off the engine. A man in a crisp white shirt and black trousers walked past. I bet that's him, she thought. She turned her head to the side, not wanting to be seen. She tried hard not to be on time but couldn't help herself.

Dennis answered the door and kissed her cheek. Come in. Come in. He leant down towards her ear. You mean you haven't had sex for ages? he whispered.

I should have known better than to tell you anything, she said and made a face.

You introduce Sofia, he said as Ingrid walked out of the kitchen wiping her hands on a towel.

In the lounge room, a group of large cushions lay on the floor in one corner. Pictures, handcrafts, tapestries from their travels gave colour and texture to the room. Dennis had said that every dollar he earned bought another kilometre of travel.

This is Keirin.

Keirin stood up and shook Sofia's hand. It was him all right. He said something to her and his eyes popped out of his head at her – with enthusiasm or wanting to please, or something. She averted her eyes.

Keirin's just moved to Sydney.

Sofia nodded and sat on the couch breathing in a familiar smell of aftershave – the kind that most men his age seemed to wear.

It's so different in the city, Keirin said. On the farm you don't have to think about what you're going to do on a Sunday. There's always a fence to mend or a horse to shoe.

Sofia's just come back from China, said Dennis, coming in from the kitchen with a tray and four glasses of red wine:

China?

I cycled across southern China.

You must be a masochist, Keirin said.

Hong Kong to Beijing by bicycle, plane and train.

If you said you'd ridden across China on a horse, I'd understand, Keirin laughed.

She told them all about the trip. How it was minus three degrees in the south and no heating and minus ten in Beijing but apart from that she had a great time. She'd booked with an adventure travel company. There were eight of them in the group including two triathletes and two bicycle couriers, so she'd ended up trailing along behind everyone.

Why did you go in the middle of winter? asked Keirin.

I wanted to be out of Sydney for the new year. I hate being alone during the holiday period and I've always wanted to see China. Maybe lose some weight too. Dennis told me I'd come back looking like a greyhound.

Everyone I spoke to didn't do much on New Year's Eve, Ingrid said. Watched the fireworks and then went to bed.

Your holiday would have been so much better if you'd had someone to cycle with, said Keirin.

Sofia shrugged.

Okay, said Ingrid. Everyone sit at the table. The food's getting cold.

The smell of garlic and prawns sizzling in oil. They sat around the wooden table under the window with the view to the west. We can see the mountains on a clear day, Dennis was fond of saying. There was a choice of butter or avocado to spread on the bread that Dennis had baked in his new bread maker.

Talking about travelling in a group reminds me of that bus trip I did to Ayers Rock, he said. It was a twenty-one-day trip. I was the only man with twenty-one women. I realised it was a perfect arrangement. I could have a different woman each night for the entire trip.

Dennis, you really are disgusting, Ingrid said.

And then there was a set of sixteen-year-old twins.

This will make you want to vomit, said Ingrid with that long-suffering look that said, we all know what Dennis's like.

They were the ones who approached me, Dennis protested. Came up and sat next to me one on either side and asked me for a hug.

Sure, Ingrid said.

It was all very innocent. We just sat there with our arms around each other. I didn't touch their boobs or kiss them.

Thanks for sharing those details with us.

Sofia passed around the bread.

Avocado, thanks, said Dennis.

I don't eat butter.

I've known you for a long time, said Keirin to Dennis. And this is the first time I've sat around at your table.

No, Keirin, That's not right. You've been here before.

But I've never sat at your table.

We go back a long way you and me.

Thirty years it must be. Since you were married the first time. And I suppose your shit still doesn't smell.

Dennis laughed and turned to Ingrid. Well, does it, Ingrid? he asked.

I don't know, she said. I've never put my nose that close to it.

No thanks, said Sofia when Dennis passed around the ice cream.

Go on, said Keirin. It's greyhound food.

Go on, said Dennis. Just a small spoonful.

I read an article saying that women go for men who are bigger and more powerful than themselves, said Sofia. Men who'll protect them. Whereas older men go for younger women who can bear children.

Apparently we choose partners on the basis of resources in exchange for physical attractiveness, said Ingrid.

Caring for a family in return for good breeding potential.

A theory that explains why rich, ugly men can still attract young, beautiful women.

Like Murdoch.

He could have found someone closer to her own age, Ingrid put in.

A man could be small and bald even and not powerful, said Dennis. But be very interesting. Say, a writer. Women would be attracted to him, wouldn't they?

Sure, said Sofia. That's true.

After dinner, Sofia showed them the photos and told them about a man named Robert.

This is something you'd like to know, Dennis, Sofia said. A bit of romance and all that. This is Robert. He was on the trip alone. We hung around together, sat next to each other at meals. I confided in him, told him how much I was suffering with the cold. I thought Robert and I might have a holiday romance in the beginning. But the closest we got was on New Year's Eve when he kissed me on the lips.

Did you wet them first? asked Dennis.

It was an unexpected kiss.

Dennis smirked.

You're so flamboyant – he was probably waiting for you to make the first move, said Ingrid.

I went to his room one night to see how his remote worked because mine wasn't working. He'd invited me in. The next morning he told the others I'd been into his room to play with his remote. They all laughed of course.

That's a bad sign, said Ingrid. That he told the others.

And then the next night after dinner when we went for a walk, he excused himself and said he had to go back to his room and write a letter home to his mother.

What nationality? Keirin asked.

English.

Well, that says it all.

I told him I was so cold I slept with all my clothes on with two doonas on top.

One time he said to the group, Who's done the most whingeing on this trip? And then he pointed to me.

Too old for you, Ingrid said. He doesn't look your type.

You've got a funny idea about a holiday, said Keirin. My idea of a holiday is to lie by a swimming pool with a martini in my hand.

Goodnight, and thanks for a great evening, said Sofia at the door.

Ingrid was behind her. What do you think of him? she whispered.

He's not my type but I'm trying to keep an open mind. Sofia touched the doorknob.

He's in denial, Ingrid said. He said he'll miss the horses but not the woman. He's going through major stuff. A marriage break-up, losing his farm. Major life change and he says it's nothing. I've tried to get him to talk but he says, It will pass soon. What would it be like living in the same house with a partner but in separate bedrooms? He told me that his wife is menopausal. She won't talk to him. He said he's not going to put so much into a relationship next time. He's not going to do that again. You have to, I said. Everyone does when they're in a relationship with another person. You put so much of yourself into it.

*

The next morning the phone rang.

How about dinner on Saturday night?

That would be nice.

I don't know where. We'll decide on the night. Spontaneity, that's the thing. It's good to be spontaneous. I'll pick you up at seven.

Keirin wearing brown leather boots to the ankle, jeans, wool flecked jacket over white shirt, slight bulge of stomach over his belt.

Let me help you out of the car, he said.

It wasn't as if she needed any help.

Don't jump out so quickly, he instructed.

She waited.

You're obedient, he said. I only had to tell you once.

In the restaurant, he kept saying how good the food was. She agreed. The food's good. Very good food.

Then silence.

There's no doubt about Dennis, Keirin said. It's a wonder Ingrid stays with him.

She has an interesting life with him. They travel together.

He touched her arm as they spoke.

That feels muscly, he said.

She flexed her biceps at him.

I don't like strong women, he said. It's very unfeminine.

Silence again.

The cutting of the bamboo began as a loud crash as one huge bamboo spear crashed against the balcony before thudding to the ground. She could see a man in a blue top up a bamboo shoot sawing it down. His white gloves flickered and his scythe flashed as she watched his young blond hair reflect in the sun.

*

You choose the gym as a place to have your next massage, not your own home where you're more vulnerable, but a public place with people around where you'll feel quite safe – an unattractive masseur this time – an older man with a lisp who you don't fancy at all. Receding white greying hair, fat lips, dressed in white. You try him out and if he seems fine you book for a series of four massages at a reduced rate.

You tell Ingrid you need to be touched and that's why you have a massage. You ask her if she removes all her clothes for the massage or leaves her underpants on. She tells you she leaves her underpants off so you think it's safe and okay when you're having a regular massage in a public place like a gym. The lower back area feels great when you stretch and pummel it, you tell him. I know a lot of us hold our anger in our buttocks, you add.

This time when he finishes your back, you say to him, Have you got time to do my chest? Yes, he says his voice a bit husky. And your tummy? Sure, you say. So there you are lying on your back having your chest massaged, under the armpits and in and under all the bits of your chest and ribs when his hand starts vibrating across the tips of your nipples very lightly. Well, you know from your daughter who's a naturopath that masseurs aren't meant to touch your nipples. Sometimes they have to touch the breasts if they get in the road of getting to the ribs, she'd said. You have to lift the breasts up and move them out of the way. Is it good for you to have your stomach massaged? you'd asked her. Yes, she said. It helps the bowel and aids digestion. A regular massage is very good for you. It helps remove the blocked-up toxins, boosts the immune system and aids against cancer by removing the stored tension in the body.

So the masseur hovers at first over your breasts and then before long he's massaging them. You remember reading in the newspaper about male doctors accused of massaging their patients' breasts and then manually bringing them to orgasm. At first you resist. You don't want to feel any expectation to perform – to have an orgasm at his instigation.

Afterwards you open your eyes and look at the clock on the wall to see how long it has all taken. You're surprised to see you've had the massage and the special extras and it's all within the allocated hour.

After you dress, the masseur says, I'd like your discretion. It's an added service that's available to you at any time for no extra charge.

You're in shock so you don't say anything. You just make a time for your next appointment and decide that next time you'll say, No special extras, thanks all the same.

*

Two weeks later Ingrid rang to say Keirin was in love. Thought you'd like to know, she said. Keirin has met a girl. He brought her over to our place. They've just left. He said he's in love. He's worried because it was so quick. It was like a blow to the back of the neck, he said. Those were his words, not mine.

Now the bamboo is cut down, Sofia can see the waves breaking on the shore again. The rhythmic rise, the white foam gathering, suspended, then breaking and tumbling into the sand of the beach. Next to her window the waterfall gushes after the rain – the drops dripping and plinking on the steel of the veranda.

Michael

He's waiting at the bottom of the ramp, just inside the steel fence that cordons off the entry to the station. He said to give him a ring from her mobile when the train passed Gosford. She quickens her pace, adjusts the overnight bag on her shoulder. She is close enough to see the soft fold of his greying hair, the clear smooth glow of his skin. In his white socks and slip-on loafers he looks very English.

It wasn't easy to get herself on a train up to the Central Coast and out of Sydney. It took a lot of encouragement on his part and a steely determination on hers. But now she's glad already that he kept pressing.

'It will do you good,' he said on the phone, 'to get out of the city for a couple of days. It will give you a new perspective on things.'

He knows about her tendency to brood and her struggle to manage the drowsiness that follows. They talk about these things on the telephone. He also struggles to get through the days, suffers with the same lethargy. He says he prefers to tell people he has chronic fatigue. People understand the term 'chronic fatigue'.

He sees the deepening of laugh lines around her mouth and eyes, her face browned by the sun, her hair spiked and in shock. He tells her that she looks the same as he remembers. She assures him he looks very well and living away from the city obviously agrees with him.

Would she like a coffee? Or would she prefer to have a shower first? Some people needed to have a shower before they could do anything.

For goodness sake. It was only a couple of hours on the train. She would like to wash her hands, though. They smelt of the tuna sandwich she'd eaten on the train.

Sure, sure. He's been waiting all day for a coffee. They'll go somewhere close by.

She'd agreed on the phone that there'd be no post-mortem. 'Don't worry,' she said. 'I'm happy to be in the present. I don't need any analysis. You're the one who goes on and on…on the telephone.'

How well she remembers that first time she had seen him. He was at one of the Saturday night dances that she used to frequent. He was standing at the side of the hall, his thick blond hair brushed back off his forehead. He'd asked her to dance, said she danced well. Then they'd met up regularly and got to know each other. He wanted them to hire a hall and practise their dance routines. 'But we mustn't get involved, you and me,' he warned. 'Too dangerous.' They were sitting in his car at the time, so close in the front seat that she could smell the Palmolive soap on his skin. She watched his hands as he put the car into gear and reversed up the driveway.

She pictures him sitting on one of the chairs that lined the edge of the Crystal Ballroom, bending down to change his shoes, his fingers tying the laces of his patent leather dance shoes. He was still young then; they both were, Michael and Sofia. She can see him there, her old dancing friend, still full of life and with plans for the future, preparing himself to come alive on the dance floor. And on the dance floor she'd surrender to his strong lead, prepared to follow wherever he took her.

Now, he opens the back door of his car and motions for her to get in. 'Sorry about the mess,' he says. 'It's easier if you sit in the back. Easier than moving all that stuff on the front seat.'

It's the same car as last time, an orangey-red Mitsubishi with scratches down the side, the same cracked glass of the headlights. She slides across the vinyl of the back seat, her eyes dazzled by a blaze of early summer sunlight passing through the spotted salt stains on the windscreen.

He puts her bag in the boot and she pushes the tapes and DVDs and beach towels a little more to the other side. She snaps on the seat belt, looks through the window at an older man in loose baggy clothes slumped on a wooden bench staring at the concrete of the pavement between his knees. She imagines she can hear his sighs.

Michael opens the window across from the driver's side as he drives, then rests his arm along the empty front passenger seat and turns to speak to her. 'Is it too windy for you?'

She reminds him his fast driving makes her nervous.

'I didn't know that. I'll slow down, now that you've told me. I'd better anyway, because I've lost my licence.'

'Again? Every time I see you, it's the same story.'

'That's a bit harsh. It's a lesson I still need to learn.'

It's like being in a taxi in a way, sitting in the back like this, not too close to the driver. A memory flashes into her mind of when she was a child and had seen a taxi parked by the side of the road. She'd looked in as she walked past. The driver had his hand between a woman's legs and the woman, an older woman, not a young woman, maybe the same age as she is now, had a funny glazed look on her face that she'd never seen before. She remembers it vividly. The man, the odd position of the two of them in the front seat, the look on the woman's face.

'How come you've lost your licence again?' she asks.

'The twelve points were up,' he says. 'You lose three points for an infringement.'

'Parking infringement?'

'No. If you get an infringement in the holiday period, they double the points, so it doesn't take much from there to get to the twelve points.'

'Speeding?'

'You've got to be very careful where the schools are, which are forty. Six double demerit points.'

With one arm resting on the ledge of the open window he runs his fingers through his hair. He'd been ringing every few weeks since they reconnected. Sometimes she tries to ring him, to save him the expense of the long telephone calls, but he's impossible to contact. It was only recently that he gave her his address. No answer machine, no mobile, no internet, and he doesn't answer the telephone. In fact, he said he pulled the phone out of its socket.

He belongs to some strange group that he won't give a name. Calls it a meditation group, but she knows it's something else. At first she thought it must be AA but now she thinks it might be some kind of a secret sect.

He honks his horn at the woman in front as they wait at a roundabout. 'This wouldn't happen in the UK,' he says. 'They don't know how to use roundabouts here.'

It was always his dream to work hard and then retire young and live somewhere by the sea.

He finds a place to park in the shade on the top floor of a shopping centre, so they can walk straight in. He takes her hand when they get out of the car.

'We're holding hands, are we?' she says. She lets him do it, passively leaves her hand in his. 'Don't forget they smell fishy.'

He shrugs.

They find a seat near the back. She had been looking forward to sitting by the water somewhere and breathing in the salt air, rather than sitting in a shopping centre, but doesn't express her disappointment.

On the phone he'd said something about telling people in the café that she's his wife. That they could read their newspapers while drinking coffee each day. She said they'd look like an old married couple if they drank coffee hidden behind their separate papers. That's when he said he'd tell everyone they were married.

'They only give you one shot of coffee at this place,' he says. 'Other cafés give you two.'

Shots? The word reminds her of the days when his drinking was out of control. Not that she knew him then.

Now that they are seated together, he says, 'I knew it would be like this. That we'd pick up from where we left off. No different from last time.'

*

How dull all sounds are by the water, she thinks. Dull but sharp, like the cheepings in the branches of the trees in front of the motel. It must be the serenity of so much water. She decided to take the motel option even though he said she could stay in the guest room at his house. His front door was broken and you had to climb in through the back, the water taps were temperamental, the sliding glass door on the shower needed to be handled just so, the carpet in front of the television only to be walked on with bare feet.

'Why don't you get the lock fixed?' she asked when they walked back out to his car.

'Not before I go away,' he said. 'When I go to Europe to visit my mother, I'll get the door fixed.'

His mother again. He's been saying for the last two years that he's going back to the UK to visit his mother.

Sofia chose to stay at the first place he showed her, a motel across the road from the beach. It was just a couple of minutes drive from his house, so they could still meet up each day. It's an upstairs room, with two beds and a view of the road and the palm trees in front.

She lay on top of the covers on the spare bed of the motel room, reading. He said if it was him, he'd sleep on that bed. You'd get more of a through breeze.

He's been to the beach for a swim. He arrived unannounced at the sliding screen door, knocked and walked in. Now he is looking at himself in the mirror in front of the bed. He turns from side to side inspecting his body, admiring his reflection, bare chest above the white shorts, says something about her being a good five years older than him.

'I'm not older than you,' she scowls. 'You say that every time. We're the same age.'

He rubs her foot a little. It doesn't really matter so much, does it? We're friends, aren't we? He was getting ready to say that they'd known each other for a long time, when she turns on him and says, 'If you say we've known each other a long time again and it doesn't matter, I'll scream.'

The family who own the motel are very friendly. The old grandfather sweeps the leaves on the driveway each morning and the grandchildren go off to school with a bang of their screen door. The children's father hands the local newspaper up to her through the railing when he sees her sitting outside her room eating breakfast. They probably watch when Michael picks her up in his car and she climbs into the back seat.

Now that she's here on his home territory, he won't go on any walks with her, won't show her where the tracks lead. Says it's best if she finds out for herself.

She says in the city she wouldn't head out on an unknown bush track on her own.

'The city,' he sighs from the front seat where she can't see his face. 'Ah…I keep thinking they'll design a new Armagnac Cognac.'

'Cognac?'

He laughs.

It's a shame he didn't take her with him when he went for a swim; she would like to know the best place to go for a dip. She's enjoying being a passenger, though, being chauffeured around.

'I tried to ring you at Christmas to see how you were going,' she says. 'I know it's a difficult time for you, with no family here. I tried at least six times – in the mornings and in the night times.'

'There's no point in ringing in the mornings,' he says. 'The phone doesn't go back on till after coffee.'

'What do you mean?'

'I take it off the hook when I go to sleep. I don't want people ringing from the other side of the world. They forget it's an eleven-hour time difference. So I don't put it back on the hook until I come back from having a coffee. I don't want the phone breaking up my morning routine. And at night time I don't come back in from the garden until after eight.'

Probably avoiding his mother. 'I've rung after eight,' she says. 'You're so hard to contact. It's a wonder you've got any friends at all. I sent you a Christmas card, by the way. Did you get it?'

He shakes his head.

'That's a shame. I sent the card to your post office box, like you said.'

'I'm going to get rid of my post box at the house. Every time the postman rides his bike up, he ruins the grass.' He sniffs deeply, with a heaving of his chest. 'When I go to the shopping centre, there's nowhere to park in the holiday period and people park on the lawns. I guess it's like that in the city.'

'Probably. I try and walk everywhere. I'm trying to lose weight.'

'That's good. Cutting back on the pasta?'

Her eyes narrow at the back of his head. 'I don't eat pasta.'

He twists around and smirks. 'That's right. You're into healthy foods.'

Back at his place he'd tried to play with her bare feet when he sat next to her on the couch. She'd pulled them away. On the bed in the motel room, he'd hugged her and wanted to lie back on the bed.

When he turns off the motor, she opens the door slowly and lets the strong salty wind flood into the car in one cool, cleansing breath.

His words are carried off into the breeze.

*

They've had an altercation, in a café down near the beach. The diamond in the nostril of the girl behind the coffee machine had flared beneath the fluorescent light. The girl was silently mouthing the words to a song playing in the background when Sofia got up and walked out.

'You should speak up sooner,' he called after her. 'You should speak up before it gets to this point.'

She has heard this before, or something like it. She turned around briefly but did not stop.

'You send knives into the heart when you speak like that,' he called. 'Sofia?'

She kept walking until she got to the bush track by the sea. She heard the echo of her own footsteps on the earth. He made her so angry. She wanted to be free of him. He made it so impossible.

'You need to be careful,' he'd said. 'Or you'll go under. All the way under.'

An insistent fly buzzed near her face.

She walks.

The track keeps weaving away from the sea and makes it difficult to keep close to the water. She has no idea where she is headed or how far she needs to go to escape her anger. Tree roots stumble away from her sandshoes. Flies buzz too close to her ears. She brings to mind a bird that she saw with friends recently. She can't recall exactly who she was with and where she was, just that someone said, 'Look at that bird. It's so big.' A black and white bird with a large wing span flying through a gorge. Maybe that's where she was? Cataract Gorge, in Launceston. Walking along that track alone, but with all those other people going in the same direction. The best part was approaching the gorge and being so surprised to see such natural beauty in the middle of a city.

She walks. After all, she's free as a bird. Her children are grown-up and lead their own lives. He always said he preferred a woman who's had children. There's something about women who've had children that he finds very appealing. The sound of the wind in the trees; the setting sun over her shoulder casts shadows on the dirt track. The sweet smell of earth. So why did she come then? She wanted to get out of Sydney, that's all. A change of scene. She needed a holiday and she didn't want to be alone.

As she moves deeper into the bush of the landscape – the ebb and the flow of the waves to her left – she begins to forget his limitations… and her own.

Loneliness. That's all.

In the mid-afternoon haze, she just feels the need to keep going, to keep moving on. When she's ready, she will go back and apologise for her behaviour. After all, they've known each other a long time.

She lets him diminish from her thoughts, and moves deeper into the tender late-afternoon light. The sea, always in motion, not too far away. She walks, and the great swelling of sound begins to recede behind her. Her feet at last on the ground.

'Put your feet on the ground, sit up with a straight back,' the counsellor had said in an attempt to get her to pull herself together. Perhaps the counsellor was uncomfortable with all the tears. But who knows? The last counsellor had let her cry, but not too much. Do they let you cry for a set period of time at those places?

She had slept with Michael only once. It took him five years to speak to her again. Five years. Later, he said something about her breasts reminding him of his mother's.

The bird sounds have softened, got gentler, more mellow. As the sun makes its slow arch, she observes the changes in the bush, what is revealed, and what is hidden. It's so peaceful she's almost afraid to breathe.

There is no specific place she is heading towards. She could stop at any time, turn around, go back. The stillness of it all. An insect flitters between the twigs.

The landscape of shrubs and trees she has been moving through is now more like a rainforest. She watches the filtered light between the long thin strands of fern. All around is a canopy of leaves – fern leaves, frond leaves, mossy leaves – bright green leaves skating on the breeze. And tree trunks: hollowed out, split in two, grooved and gnarled.

She looks up. In what direction are the clouds travelling? She's lost her bearings. She forgot to look for the position of the setting sun before she entered the forest. It is so hot. She is sweating.

But as she walks on, she is happy in her own self. In a new self, not the old one that she's left behind.

She looks back the way she's come.

Is she lost?

She reminds herself not to panic and, standing there absorbing the landscape, breathes in deeply to the count of four, and then out again … four, three, two, one.

She sees another insect on a roller coaster with the air. The web of a spider made visible in the glow.

In the humidity and sleepy afternoon light, she could keep going forever, all the way back to Sydney.

Henry Again

'No capacity for emotional intimacy' is how Ingrid likes to describe Henry.

I told her that he had been emailing me about coming over to play dress-ups. It was raining so hard on the flat roof above us, where we sat drinking coffee at a café by the harbour, that I had to raise my voice to tell her about it.

It was early evening on a Friday that he rang and asked if he could come over. An autumn evening and not too cold for Henry and me to be sitting around in our lingerie in my lounge room.

'He's a good-looking bloke, Ingrid. Well, you've seen him. He's not everyone's cup of tea but I like him. His biceps are large and well defined and his back muscles bulge, probably from all that paddling on his surfboard. He's a volunteer lifesaver, you know?'

Ingrid nodded and took a sip of coffee.

'Anyway, he brought all the gear. I told him on the phone that if he wants me to dress up to bring the stuff. Every time he comes over, he says we need to look through my underwear drawer, but I keep telling him I haven't got anything much. One day I'll get some of those things. I said he could buy them for me or lend me his. "But I'm bigger than you," I pointed out. "That's part of the fun," he told me. "Fitting you into it." He stood behind me to dress me up. Lace-up bustier, cream waisted French silk knickers, garter belt, white sheer stockings, and then a silk loose open gown on top. I pulled myself in with my hands like you see in the old movies while he did me up.

'He'd brought a DVD for us to watch – *Pleasantville*. I'd asked him to bring some music and I said I'd provide the candles. He likes to get the atmosphere right. And he's very fussy about what he listens to. The movie was good. It showed people living in a bland colourless world behind a traditional facade contrasted with a new world where it was accepted for them to be free to be themselves and to express their individuality.'

'Sounds heavy.' Ingrid blew on her coffee, sipped it.

'Light and funny. But I couldn't follow the action of the story very well because he kept distracting me. He sat me on his lap and he was behind me. At least with my back to him I wouldn't risk laughing at the sight of him dressed in women's underwear.'

'So what was he wearing? Did he look like Frank-N-Furter?'

'He was in soft colours like me, cream bustier, garter belt, silk undies, white sheer stocking and a turquoise silk over-jacket. I couldn't really see much and I didn't want to look. I didn't notice if he arrived in the same sandals with a heel that he wore the first time. He'd said then, "Why shouldn't a man make himself look taller?"'

Ingrid screwed her face up into a frown. 'And make-up?'

'His hair was tied back in a bun, not hanging loose and full to his shoulders like last time. He doesn't wear lipstick or nail polish, not with me anyway.'

'I'd hate that.' Ingrid wound her scarf more securely around her neck as the rain kept up its pounding.

'It was sort of fun. I didn't much like the feel of his padded bra sticking into my chest when later he climbed into my bed and we hugged each other under the doona. That's when I found myself clutching at his biceps with my eyes closed wanting to feel the maleness of his upper body. I don't know what was going on lower down, under his garter belt. I let him control the moves. "If you want to get me into the bedroom, you'll have to look like a man," I said that first time. That night he went into another room and took off all the women's underwear that he'd worn under his clothes and returned looking fairly normal. His androgynous-looking normal – his shoulder-length hair in a ponytail, his hairless body, his small head. I've said it before: he thinks of himself as a male lesbian. He's not interested in men.'

Ingrid had finished her coffee and she leant back in the chair. 'Male lesbian? That's a funny thing to say.'

'It makes sense. He looks like a man but wants to dress as a woman. A lesbian in drag. Anyway, after the movie – it must have been about ten or eleven by then – I went to the bathroom and when I came out I found him in bed already with the doona pulled up under his chin. I hopped in with all the gear on and we hugged and kissed. I kept gripping at his skin, at the mass of his body, the parts of him that weren't covered with the underwear. I remember wanting to feel chunks of his flesh under my hands.'

'Yuck, Sofia. That's disgusting.'

'It's a fetish, that's all. I didn't much like the musty smell, or old smell, or unwashed smell, or whatever it was, of the vintage clothing. I tried to concentrate on other things, the nice things that were happening. He takes his time. It was midnight and he was finally lying on top of me when his mobile rang. Some computer glitch. I was annoyed he answered it.'

Ingrid's eyebrows raised enquiringly, 'So he makes love like a man?'

'Both. I asked him once if he was planning to have his penis cut off but he laughed and said, "It still comes in handy."'

Ingrid giggled, then pressed her lips firmly together.

'After the phone call, we simply lay back on the pillows. I felt very tired by then. He was talking and talking, maybe telling me some more about his trip to the UK and his travels in his motor home to dance venues all over England and then to Normandy in his military gear to role play D-Day. He'd emailed me a photo of himself in full army uniform with a rifle and there he was emerging from the jungle. An odd photograph from a man who looks so unmasculine. I'd assumed he was trying to make himself more macho and it wasn't until he returned that I found out he's a historic re-enactor. Part of a worldwide group who replay world wars dressed in all the gear.'

'A transgender re-enactor?' Ingrid put in.

'No labelling, remember? Before he left for the UK, he told me how his suitcase was full of old military uniforms. He was so excited he'd found jackets with their original buttons still intact and authentic hats to complete the outfits. Anyway, his voice was going on and on in a monotone and I was lying back absolutely exhausted – totally knackered.

'My eyes must have been closing for seconds at a time because he said, "You're tired. I'll go home."

'That's when I said, "You can stay the night if you like."

'"I know you like to have the mornings to yourself," he said.'

Ingrid zipped her parker up to just under her chin. In front of us the rain had enveloped the apartment blocks at Double Bay in a shroud of watery mist. The rain still so loud we couldn't hear the waves unfurling on the shore on the bay below us.

'So, what happened then?'

'He got out of bed and I got out of bed and we took off all our vintage underwear and he packed it in his bag. He said I could keep the stockings, though. He'd bought them new but his legs are longer than mine. "It'll need a wash," I said referring to the underwear as I stepped out of it. I didn't ask him to help undo all the clips on the back of the bustier. Much less romantic than when he'd laced me up earlier in the evening.'

The area around Ingrid's mouth had come over all tight and wrinkled. She pushed her empty cup away and crossed her arms in front of her chest. 'So when will you see him again?'

I shrugged and shook my head. 'I don't know. I told him about Tim. How Tim and I had lunch that same day and how Tim had said on the bus on the way home, "I suppose there's no chance of a root?" "Ask me again when your broken ribs have healed," I said. I was telling Henry about the meeting with Tim. "It can be done," said Henry. "It's possible to have sex with broken ribs." And then he said, "So Tim knows you're up for it then?"

'I was only joking, I said. Tim is a big drinker. But the funny thing is I nearly had a double booking tonight, between you and Tim.'

Ingrid snickered.

'Henry told me to stay away from drinkers. He doesn't drink or smoke, Ingrid. He hates all alcohol and drugs.'

She nodded and her perfectly bobbed and blonded hair bounced against the side of her face.

'He probably thinks Tim and I are an item now. I must give him a ring and see if he's going to the Music and Dance Festival. They usually invite him to come with his dance partner and they give an exhibition and run some workshops.'

'He does look fantastic on the dance floor, I must say,' said Ingrid. 'He puts on quite a performance.'

'My dancing friend Edward – you know, very tall Edward – said he's seen Henry and his dance partner at the festival many times. Edward said she's Henry's wife. But I know she's not. Henry hasn't got a wife. I asked Henry once where he stays when he goes to the festival He said in his motor home with his dance partner and they park it down near the river.'

'Does he sleep with her?'

'I want to ask him that but haven't. He's not very good with the personal questions.'

The rain eased in front of us at the café and the apartment blocks emerged looking all clean and bright.

'I wondered if that night of the dress-ups was the end of it between him and me. Mission accomplished. He'd wanted me to accept him dressed as a woman in the bedroom and I'd done it. He packed all the stuff up, except the stockings, and went home. It was only after he left I realised I'd forgotten to get the candles out.'

Ingrid looked out and across the water. 'I must buy myself a bustier,' she said in a wistful voice.

We stayed sitting there for a long time until the raindrops on the roof had slowed and steadied. Two seagulls danced in and out in between the sails of the yachts that were anchored in the bay.

The Spa

'When are you open?' Sofia asks the woman on the telephone.

'We have a party twice a day. Every day. Twelve-thirty to four-thirty and seven-thirty to midnight.'

'Oh. Every day? I thought it was Saturday nights only.'

'No, darling. Every day.'

'So what's the set-up?'

'A hundred and twenty dollars for a couple. Nothing if you come on your own. What's your position? How would you come along?'

'On my own.'

'It would cost you nothing then.'

'But what do you do? I mean, I know what goes on there.'

'You've been here before?'

'No. A friend told me about it. What do you wear? What's the set-up?'

'It's all up to you, love. If you fancy a gentleman, you invite him into one of the rooms.'

'What do you wear, though? My friend said something about robes.'

'Towels. They're towels, love. You wear whatever you like. Normal clothes.'

Sofia and Ingrid are having breakfast by the beach. Scrambled tofu for Sofia and fried eggs and bacon for Ingrid.

I'm dying to know how you went, Ingrid says, pulling her chair closer to the table.

Well, Sofia says, this is what happened.

It's about eight-thirty on Saturday night when I approach a big steel gate with a street number in bold letters. I open the gate and go up the lane way beside the Thai restaurant and follow the fairy lights upstairs.

There's nothing else to indicate what goes on inside this three-bedroom apartment on a busy road in Bondi. I follow the fairy lights along a corridor until I come to a wooden front door with no number on it. I hesitate not knowing whether to knock or just walk in. I open the door.

Inside, draped around the room, are about ten men and women in various stages of undress sitting on stools beside small bar tables – the men bare-chested, the women topless or wearing bras. Some of them are giving each other neck and shoulder massages. And they're all wearing towels. Not a very attractive sight, in my opinion – a man in a towel.

It's a large room with a pretend bar, a kitchen on the right and sliding glass doors that lead to a covered balcony with an above-ground spa pool. Standing by the door are two Japanese men in black jeans and black T-shirts. I walk over to the kitchen, which acts as the reception area.

The only other fully dressed people in the room are the man and the woman who run the place. She's Czech, young and very attractive in a green lace figure-revealing dress. Her blonde hair cascades down her back. She's in the kitchen and doesn't exactly greet me but asks me what I'd like to drink. A glass of wine would be nice, I say. She goes to the fridge and from a cask on the bottom shelf pours me a glass. With drink in hand, I stand near the door and look around. And wonder what I'll do next.

The two Japanese men avoid eye contact with me. They obviously want to keep to themselves. I don't particularly want to join the group of men and women on the stools as I don't intend to take any of my clothes off.

I ask the woman who runs the place to show me around. She shrugs without much enthusiasm then leads the way along a narrow hallway. The first bedroom on the right has a double bed with a bedside light on a table and white lace curtains on the window. She looks out between the lace peering around outside before pulling them closed.

She shows me another bedroom at the end of the corridor with an en suite bathroom. We stand at the door looking in to the empty bed but she doesn't show me in. And then she leads the way to the third bedroom back along the corridor towards the front door. This is the Orgy Room, she says from the open doorway.

I avert my eyes but I can see from the corner of one eye a double bed and several naked bodies doing things to each other. Backs and thighs and bums exposed. Not very becoming. It all seems tacky and I begin to doubt my wisdom in coming to a place like this. I clutch my handbag across my body and find myself a seat in the front room with my back to the wall.

There are corn chips and an onion dip on a platter that the women in the group hand around. I decline the chips and the dip. If there's one thing I can't stand, it's the smell of onion breath.

A woman in a white lace bra and a towel around her waist stubs out her cigarette in the ashtray in front of me and asks if I've been here before.

No, I say. And you?

I come here all the time. What do you do for a living? she continues.

A bit of this and that.

She nods knowingly.

What do you do? I ask.

I'm a psychologist at a clinic at St Leonards.

I'm very surprised. For some reason, I thought women with important jobs wouldn't come to a place like this.

A man edges over towards me and tries to get in on our conversation. He asks the same things as she does. Do you come here often? What do you do for a living?

In the old days, or rather in the olden days, as my children like to say, when I used to frequent bars from time to time, I'd answer the first question with 'only in the mating season' and the second question with 'I live off the income from my investments'. Both replies would be met with a stunned silence or an impressed 'ah' or, sometimes, 'is this the mating season?'

The man keeps smiling at me and I avert my eyes but somehow he is able to manoeuvre himself around so he's constantly in my line of vision. It gives me the shits.

Not your type? Ingrid puts in.

No. Absolutely not.

What did you wear in the end? Ingrid asks.

Only four items of clothing.

Something you could take off quickly?

Yes. And no jewellery. Apparently the men have to shower and put on a towel as soon as they arrive. Although one woman kept saying to me, Where's your towel? She wanted me to get undressed and hang about in a towel like everyone else.

Another woman tells me I should leave my bag locked up in the kitchen with the man and woman who own the place.

You don't know these men, cautions the woman. Lock up your bag.

I decide to keep my bag with me although I've left my umbrella beside the door. Another man edges his stool over towards me and we have a conversation. At least he's got a brain in his head and got something to say for himself.

He tells me he's Dutch and he's here in Sydney on business. It's my first time to this place, he says. But I've been to others in other cities in the world. I travel a lot for business.

We talk a little about travel and countries we've visited.

He lets me know in a non-threatening way that he'd be willing to go into one of the bedrooms with me. I feel embarrassed knocking him back, seeing as we've had such a nice conversation and I don't want him to be wasting time with me if he wants to be chatting up some other woman.

I'm not ready, I say politely. Maybe later.

The other man who's been trying to catch my eye, the pain-in-the-bum-persistent-dag who listens in to my every word, leans over towards me and says, When you're ready, would you go into one of the rooms with me?

No thanks, I say. Sorry, I smile at him, hoping all the same that I haven't hurt his feelings.

The Dutch man tells me there's no need to apologise.

A few new people wander in. A man and a woman, a couple, a few single men of various ages and shapes and a fat girl draped in layers of chiffon. Then two very well-proportioned young men. I remind myself that I'm the one meant to be doing the choosing here. One of the very well-proportioned young men is quite cute, actually. The other young man is not very tall, a bit too muscle-bound for my taste, and has that short spiky hair almost shaved at the side that I find most unattractive. The two of them are younger than both my sons – but that's nothing new.

One of the women ushers them out into the back bedroom to shower and put on a towel. They don't return to the main room where I'm sitting jammed up between various men and in front of me a blank video screen high up on the wall. The fat girl does some sort of disco dance in front of the wall under the video screen. She dances in time to the music but nothing special. Then the woman who owns the place uses her remote to turn on a video.

I've never seen such an explicit porn video before, Ingrid. I can't watch but I glimpse the extreme close-ups of women's genitalia and pierced intimate body parts and things being stuck in and up and it's all too horrible.

Why didn't you go home then? asks Ingrid.

I thought I'd wait just a bit longer. It had taken such an enormous effort of will to get there.

The Czech blonde who runs the place with her Indian husband enjoys the video immensely.

Look at that, she keeps saying.

I have nowhere to turn my head. In front of me the video, to my left the persistent dag. To my right is the smaller young muscly man who now also keeps trying to attract my attention, but I'm claustrophobic and I just want out of there but for some reason I'm stuck to my seat. I don't want to stand up and have everyone look at me – anything that moves is closely observed in this room. I look at the floor, at the space between my stool and the spa area, and the floor towards the front door. I'm willing myself to stand up, to walk into the spa room away from these men, or straight out the front door.

So that's how come I end up talking to the young Italian muscly bloke. He reaches his hand out to me and invites me to sit in the spa room with him away from the noise of the video. I use his hand to stand up but then remove it from his grasp before walking outside to the balcony. I don't want to look as if I've been claimed.

I tell the muscly Italian man that the men here are too predatory and I'm feeling guilty because I keep knocking them back and then find myself apologising.

You don't have to say you're sorry when you knock someone back, he assures me.

But I'm finding him intimidating right now wedged up beside me and I don't know how to get rid of him.

We sit on the black vinyl lounge, me squashed in the corner. The tang of chlorine from the empty spa assaults my nostrils.

Can I kiss your cheek? he asks.

No.

Can I hold your hand? he says.

No. I wedge my hand that lays beside him under my thigh, making sure he can't hold it.

His friend, the cutie, comes out through the door and sits beside us. We smile at each other.

I was very nervous before coming to this place, he says to me. I nearly didn't come.

I look into his open face and his nice round eyes and thick head of curly hair.

It was the same for me, I say.

When I came in, he says, I saw you sitting there and that woman in the green dress and I thought this looks all right and so I came in.

She's very attractive, I say. That woman in the green dress.

I asked her husband if she participates but he said no.

Do you think it's good value for money here? I ask in order to keep the conversation going. I mean, it's concerning me that the men have paid $180 each to come into this place and it's free for me.

No, he says, I don't think I've got good value for money. Not so far.

His friend puts his hand on my leg. I consider removing his hand but think it may seem churlish of me so I don't. And anyway, if I've come to a place like this, what am I doing knocking all the blokes back?

What does it cost to have sex with a hooker? I ask the cutie.

He looks at me with horrified wide eyes. I don't know. I've never had sex with a hooker.

I was just trying to do a price comparison, I say. A value for money price comparison. How many women have you had sex with tonight? I persist.

Two. One on arrival. A woman started massaging me when I had a shower and then we had sex. And then a second one almost straight afterwards. The fat girl.

How was that? I ask. How was the sex?

She had big bruises all over her body as if she'd been bashed up or drugs or something. Her arms and legs were all bruised. It was awful. I wished I was unconscious.

I nod with sympathy. I noticed you go into the bedroom with the fat girl, I say.

He smiles at me and extends his hands towards me, palms upturned. I could give you a great massage, he says with enthusiasm. I've got very strong hands. I'm trained in martial arts.

Mm, I say breathing out with a sigh. But the problem is I can't get rid of his bloody friend. He's latched on to me and has territorial control with his bloody hand resting on my thigh.

There are six of us in the spa room now. The cutie, his friend, a middle-aged Maori couple and the Indian husband of the Czech woman. I'd noticed some of the girls flirting with the Indian husband and then laughing. He stays close by the side of his wife. Now, though, he chats to us.

We've only had this business for eight weeks, he says. We took it over from the previous owner who'd been here for six and a half years. It costs us a thousand dollars a month in rent and a thousand for advertising on the web, in the *Telegraph* and in the *Wentworth Courier*. It isn't easy to make money.

We talk about business and making money for a while then he leaves us to it.

Do you think some of those girls are being paid to be here? asks the Italian.

Prostitutes?

Well, why would a single woman come to a place like this? says the cutie, who's disappointed there aren't more women here. A single woman can go out any time and pick up a bloke at a pub.

I don't say anything. I don't say it's probably safer here than to take a stranger home or to go back to his place in the middle of nowhere. And what are you meant to do anyway if you don't have a boyfriend?

He complains that when he rang up to make inquiries they told him there's a huge spa that fits twenty people. They could fit about eight people in this spa, he says. And even then it would be squashed. Twenty people – they'd all be on top of each other.

I must say that when my friend Richard, who told me about the place, mentioned that there was a large spa I did imagine a Grecian-type setting with women and men reclining and relaxing around the edges of the water.

If he was a good businessman, says the Cutie, he'd offer to give us our money back at the door. That's how you do business. Keep the customers happy.

There's no privacy in the rooms here, says the Italian. People walk in all the time. The Japanese men paid $50 each just to watch.

We had to jam towels up against the door to stop people walking in, says the Maori husband.

Now that the Maori couple have joined in the conversation, I use the opportunity to ask them how they're going. What they've experienced so far. I'd noticed them come out of the bedroom at the end of the house.

The wife tells me in a quiet voice that they went into the room with another woman to have a threesome. But it didn't work out, she says. He couldn't do any good, she says, indicating with a nod her husband's lap and the area between his legs. We don't like it much here. We've been to other adult clubs where it's all couples. Much better. Not with all these men hanging around staring at you.

Why did you come here? I ask.

He wants to have sex with other women, she answers. So coming to a place like this, he's not doing it behind my back. I know what he's up to and I'm included.

Her husband glows smugly.

Why did you come here? I ask the cutie.

Curiosity. Why did you come here? he asks me.

Curiosity. We all came here for curiosity, I say, summing up the conversation.

The Italian muscle-man gets up to go to the toilet. Save me that space beside you, he instructs me. Promise, he adds loudly.

I nod.

When he leaves the room, I ask the cutie if he's been into the Orgy Room.

No, he says. What Orgy Room?

It's up the hallway. I had a look around when I arrived. But an Orgy Room isn't something I'm interested in trying.

Me either, he agrees.

I'm just waiting for him to finish with you, he says, indicating the empty seat between us, and then I'll be next.

I lower my eyes discreetly and suppress a smirk.

The Italian returns from the toilet and takes his seat between us.

The cutie turns to me and says, You can give him a massage, indicating his friend, and I'll give you a massage.

I laugh.

The Maori couple encourage me from the sidelines. Go on, says the Maori husband. Give it a go. If you don't like it, leave.

Sure, I think to myself. As if I'd be able to leave after going into a bedroom with two men and taking off all my clothes. Although I wouldn't mind going in to one of the rooms with the cutie – if I could lock the door, that is, and if it wasn't so late already.

I giggle nervously. I have four people on my case now trying to persuade me to go with the two young men, as if it's my responsibility to keep everybody happy. Hoping they'll understand and lay off, I tell them I'm laughing because I'm nervous.

Would a drink calm you down? says the husband.

No, thanks.

His wife smiles at me. In a gentle voice she says, Would you like me to calm you down?

Thank you very much, but no, I say, feeling guilty as usual.

Her husband makes some more noises along the lines of the two of them could help me out with my nervousness problem.

I sigh and then stand up brushing the hand off my leg. I walk over to the side of the spa where the cutie is standing.

I ease two fingers into the water as if to test the temperature. Warm, I say.

Not warm enough, he says.

I move towards him then lift the corner of his towel to just above his knee. I dry my fingers.

His friend jumps up from the lounge and moves in front of me with his bare hairy back just inches from my face.

My back is cold, he says. Warm me up, he commands.

I hold out one hand and lay it briefly on his shoulder, then take it away.

Let's go for a walk, he whispers to me.

No, thanks.

Give me your phone number and we'll meet up another time, then.

No.

Why not?

I don't want to. I laugh nervously. How I hate these situations I find myself in.

I'm now wedged into the corner of the spa room. My eyes fix on the door. I hesitate, wondering whether I should be polite and say anything to the Maori couple. But I feel the need for haste. I'm worried he'll follow me, although a man in a towel isn't going to get very far outside on the street.

Ingrid adds butter and a sprinkle of salt to her Turkish bread and then mops up the remains of her egg yolk and the slimy gleam of the bacon fat And then?

That's it. I leave.

There was a full moon that night. The silver glistened and vibrated on the sea as Sofia neared the northern end of the beach on her walk back home. She passed the Bondi RSL club, the Bidigal reserve and the single Bondi sandhill up on her left. There weren't many people around at that hour. Heading along Campbell Parade, it was quiet. The pub and the cafés were closed.

The surf was big, the waves crashed dramatically over the rocks, the reef and the swimming pool at the south end of the beach. In Notts Avenue, she stopped at the surf viewing area just before the baths and watched the rising swell of the ocean for a few moments. She continued along Bondi Road, walking fast up the hill, pleased the steepness didn't faze her, not panting, managing it nice and easy, even in her high heels. She crossed at the lights near the pub on the corner.

A cold wind blew and then it began to rain.

She passed the laneway on her right and was heading for the shortcut home. She planned to cross the open car park of the block of units, and then down through the little park that leads to the hole in the fence that usually gets her home in no time. It was not until she was in the empty car park that she heard her own footsteps squelching on the wet surface and realised that there was another set of sounds behind her. Her shoes made a squench, squash noise and that's why she didn't realise at first what the other sound was – and that the sound had been there for some time.

'The man had a gruff, heavily accented Australian voice, his face was masked with a dark balaclava and he wore dark-coloured tracksuit pants – the same description given by his first two victims. His threats, including that he was armed with a knife, were similar to words spoken in the first two attacks and appeared well rehearsed. After each attack, he casually walked away.'

Sofia veered left as she changed course and retraced her steps without turning towards the footsteps. After moving some distance away and towards the safety of the lights of the units and a door that she could bang on in case of emergency, she turned round to see if the person was still there. He was there all right. In joggers, tracksuit, medium height, average build. He'd stopped at the point where she veered left and was looking down into the empty park.

Sorry, she thought she heard him say as he looked over towards her.

She turned and hurried back towards the road and the street lights, leaving him behind. She walked on the side of the road towards the oncoming traffic just like she did when she was on her solitary travels in Europe and the man receded into the distance.

Ingrid's plate looks so shiny clean now after her mop-up with the Turkish bread, it's as if the dish has come straight out of the dishwasher. Sofia tells her that before she went out that night she'd worried that she'd feel tacky when she got home.

You would have if you'd gone against your instincts and allowed those people to talk you into doing something you didn't want to do, Ingrid says.

I feel bad, though, that this whole sex thing is such an issue for me when there's all the killing going on in different parts of the world, and starvation and hurricanes and tsunamis and the paralympians in wheelchairs on the television every night.

You're not going around complaining, Ingrid says. You're doing something about it. It's better than those singles dances. I only went to a couple before I met Dennis, but I felt like a lump of meat being looked up and down.

But I'm such a wimp, Sofia says.

No, you're not. You went. You're not a wimp if you can go.

I'm a wimp when it comes to getting rid of guys. Some boring man always latches on to me and I end up leaving just to get rid of him or some man attempts to follow me home.

Sofia breathes out heavily and tells Ingrid that Richard was the one who'd told her about the place.

You know Richard, the one I met on the internet.

You met him in a chat room?

No, not a chat room, Sofia says, sensing Ingrid's disapproval. There are all sorts of loonies in chat rooms. No. A singles website. Richard said the women at these clubs do the choosing and there'd be lots of young men for me to pick from and plenty who'd want to give me a massage. In fact, I got so excited about the idea of me doing the choosing that I'd look at the men in the gym and sitting on the train and I'd think, would I choose you if you were there? Richard offered to come with me as my partner but why would I want to pay a hundred and twenty dollars to go as a couple when I can go for nothing? And anyway, I wouldn't want to see Richard with another woman.

It wasn't very complimentary to you that Richard offered to go with you, Ingrid says, a harsh satisfaction in her voice.

Sofia can see that telling her this about Richard pleases Ingrid.

Ingrid pouts her lips to apply a tangerine lipstick. The lipstick matches her perfectly manicured toenails that reveal themselves at the end of her stiletto sandals. She puts the lipstick away in her handbag, sits back and looks out to the ocean, then twists her wedding ring around her finger.

It's a can that I've always wanted to open, Ingrid says. To see what goes on in these places.

She stands up decisively and pulls her T-shirt down at the sides accentuating the waistless bulge of her torso that protrudes for some distance from her body. She slides her hands up and down over her stomach like a proud pregnant woman, but Ingrid isn't pregnant.

She thrusts her shoulders back and her chest out. Who cares if my gut hangs out, she says proudly. I've got a gorgeous husband, two mortgages and a great business. What more could a girl want?

Sofia feels depressed. But she won't tell her that. She's said enough already.

Amanda

'It's dreadful what happened,' my friend Amanda says with a shake of her head. 'It was my worst nightmare.'

The two of us are standing beside her car outside my motel room about to drive back to Sydney after the Music and Dance Festival.

She's composing a very long text message to Louis, the guy she was bonking in her tent last night. Was it his wife who burst in? No, no his wife is back in Sydney. It was Jim – in the middle of everything. He unzipped the flap of her tent at three in the morning and just assumed he could get into her sleeping bag again.

'Jim lurched in drunk,' she says, her thumbs jabbing and bouncing across her mobile.

'What did you do?'

'I told him to get the fuck out of there.'

'And did he?'

'Yes, he staggered out. But that was the end of it with Louis. He couldn't get away quick enough.'

Louis is her piano teacher. She's had the hots for him for ages. His wife has stopped coming to watch Louis's trio perform and she doesn't bother with the music festivals either, but his grown-up daughter does – though not this year. Still, it took Amanda three bottles of red to finally get Louis into her tent and under the sleeping bag.

'Poor Louis,' she says as she presses the send button and slumps into the driver's seat. 'He told me I'm the first woman he's kissed apart from his wife in thirty-seven years.'

I'd seen her pre-erected on-site tent. It was part of Tent City, lined up ready to go. She said it was like sleeping in a zoo, the snoring was so loud each night. Inside were two single canvas beds and two thin mattresses.

She'd taken the mattresses off the beds and laid them on the floor side by side and put her sleeping bag on top. Her clothes stayed neatly in a suitcase in the corner.

'Remember the day before, after Roger had been in my tent?' she says. 'I made sure in the morning that everything was back to normal in case Jim came back that day. And he did. He knocked on my tent flap looking for his car keys. He didn't know whose tent he'd left them in. At least he knocked that time before barging in.'

'So that's three blokes in four nights?'

She frowns as she straps on her seat belt. 'I'm not usually like this.'

I click myself in and look across at her. 'It's funny, all these people away from home – in and out of each other's tents every night.'

'You've got to grab it when it's there, that's what I think.'

The festival took over most of the huge area of the showground. Performance venues, camping space and a huge parking area. As well as international and local performers, there was a big dance floor for the opening night ball. In previous years, Amanda had stayed with friends nearby. I booked in to a motel within walking distance.

I was very pleased when she'd offered to give me a lift from Sydney. She said it would be fun to have someone to chat to on the long car journey. But for weeks beforehand I couldn't contact her to confirm the arrangement. She must have been chasing up some new bloke. In the end, we left much later than planned and arrived long after the sun had set. It wasn't easy to locate her tent in the dark. But still she managed to make it to the tail end of the Welcome Ball and to chat some guy up in the session bar afterwards. I needed to get my bearings before walking alone at night across the paddock, so missed out on going to the opening night festivities.

In the car on the way to the festival, Amanda had described her stable of men. About six. All casuals. The understanding was that there were no expectations. The latest was the roofing man who'd come to fix the leak that was dripping into her dining room. He came back after a week of rain to make sure the place was still dry.

She says she takes whatever comes her way. The way she looks at it is she's a single woman and free to do whatever she likes. 'Why shouldn't I?' she said. 'As long as they're not married.'

I don't say anything about Louis's married status – but is she deluding herself or is she in fact a liar?

Amanda and I met a few years ago through Ingrid. I can still remember my first impression of her. She was standing by the door of the Crystal Ballroom in an attitude I was going to get to know as an Amandaism – her back arched and large chest pushed forward.

'I've got big bazookas,' was how she liked to describe herself. 'And why not show off your best assets?'

She was dressed in skinny hipster jeans with a low-slung leopard print belt, purple tank top and big mop of thick dark curls hanging to her shoulders.

She turns the key in the ignition and starts up the Subaru. 'Ingrid won't be pleased with me.'

'Why not? I've never heard her speak disparagingly of you.'

'I know she won't be happy when I tell her. You wouldn't be like that. You would only do it for love.'

I redden with anger. It isn't as if I haven't had my fair share of adventures. 'I've never said anything like that. Those words would never have passed my lips. What about Henry? The guy with a ponytail. We get together every now and then.'

'So that's still happening?'

'He made it clear from the beginning that he likes to fly solo.'

'Are you happy with that?'

'No. But what can I do?'

It's a telephone conversation with Ingrid a few weeks later on a rainy winter's morning that gets me thinking about Amanda again.

'Just as well you and Amanda weren't sharing,' Ingrid says.

'It took her three bottles of red to get Louis into the tent. And then Jim came bursting in.'

'So you mean it wasn't consummated?'

'Doesn't sound like it. Jim put an end to that.'

'Shame she didn't throw a few guys your way.'

I hear Ingrid's laughter on the other end of the phone. 'I don't want that,' I say. 'It's not hard to get a bloke if that's all you want.'

The wind blows the bare branches of a tree against the window with a nasty scraping sound like fingernails down a blackboard.

'Did you say anything to her on the drive back about Louis being married?' Ingrid asks.

'I restrained myself. Apparently he felt dreadful about the whole episode. He still comes to her place, though, to play the piano. She said they've agreed it's best if they're friends only.'

'That won't be the end of it – if they didn't go all the way. She won't leave it at that.'

'I wonder why she's like that? Three blokes in four nights. She doesn't seem to be very fussy about the guys she chooses.'

'Desperation? Desperate to be loved?'

'I don't get the impression that she's desperate.'

'Neither do I.'

'Maybe she's got a voracious sexual appetite.'

'Maybe.'

I touch the icy surface of the glass and look at my own reflection in the rain-splattered window. Too generous with her body. That's what someone said to me once.

The peak-hour traffic whooshes past on the main road in front of where I sit. Is life passing me by?

I stay there at the window as the morning sun makes its slow arch towards the west and the throbbing of the morning rush hour gradually eases.

Vladimir

Dispensed with like a lump of offal. That's what it felt like. I hadn't been really. What I had done, though, was show him I have boundaries and limits. Well, that's what Ingrid said when I told her I'd been dumped by Vladimir.

'Don't say he dumped you,' she said. 'It's so negative. It's not true anyway.'

'It's over.'

'It never really began,' she scoffed.

We were walking with Ingrid's dog by the golf course, just across the road from the harbour. It was a hot and steamy morning – too hot, really, to be out exercising. At least a tiny breeze blew across the back of our necks.

'I could never go out with a man who's a drinker,' Ingrid said. 'There are many things I could compromise on, especially if there's a strong physical attraction – even different political views. But I couldn't stand it if someone drank heavily.'

'I know you don't like Russians.'

'It's only the uneducated ones.'

'He got a degree before he came out here.'

'He's a user. You're attractive. You've got your own place…you don't need it.'

Across the road golfers manoeuvred wheeled buggies around the contours of the greens. With suntanned legs, they practised their swings, then sliced the ball up the hill, before pushing their carts up the gentle slopes.

I remembered Vladimir's elongated, lean body, the deep grooves in the sides of his face, the dark shadows under his eyes, the cigarette hanging from his fingers. He was the tiredest-looking, thinnest man I had ever known. Everything about him looked haggard. When I opened the door to him that last time, I noticed how his hair had softened into curls – thick waves that changed the severity of the angles of his face.

'Baryshnikov,' he said once. 'People say I remind them of Baryshnikov, or Nureyev.'

I liked the look of him and the smell of him – I didn't mind the lingering aroma of tobacco – and I found his deep thickly accented voice very sexy.

Ingrid's dog strained against his leash as he pulled her forward. 'Dogs are a great way to meet people.'

'You promised me you wouldn't say that again,' I snapped. 'If you tell me to get a dog again, I'll scream.'

Ingrid moved ahead as Louis dragged her towards the little beach on the harbour. There was wild delight in the movement of his tail at the prospect of a splash in the sea. 'You can borrow mine,' she called out.

'I prefer people to animals.'

'A pet,' she laughed. 'He wanted to be a pet. He wanted to move in and be looked after.'

We crossed the road with the dog and headed up O'Sullivan Road by the green of the old golf course that was protected by a row of Norfolk Pines. A high mesh fence enclosed the western perimeter of the course and its rolling freeway rose and fell to perfection – the grass exquisitely manicured.

I'd said to Ingrid, not long after I met Vladimir, that I thought she'd be pleased I was finally seeing someone. She'd known him for years. They'd met at the Crystal Ballroom, long before I was introduced to him.

Ingrid and I were lunching together when I told her that Vladimir and I had started dating. I looked across the table at my friend. Devoid of make-up, she appeared pale and flat, her cornflower yellow hair pulled back severely revealing a line of grey. So different from the photograph that Dennis kept in his wallet – Dennis, my old uni friend. The marriage had its problems. Parallel lives, was how Amanda described it.

Ingrid is someone who likes to walk quickly as if wanting to arrive first at every destination. Her face is evenly constructed, her brow well-defined, her mouth set, and her eyes look off into the distance as if unable to give her attention to the person in front of her. She possesses an impatience for the moment, unwilling to empathise with people's problems when she has more than enough of her own.

'Vladimir hasn't worked for as long as I've known him,' she said one day at lunch as she stirred her miso soup with chopsticks. She scraped the last of the seaweed from her bowl. 'Has he seen your place yet?'

No, he hadn't. Not at that stage.

I was living at that time in a 1920s white stucco building on four levels, with black wrought-iron railings and lead-light windows that in the late afternoon threw dark patterns on the floor. I liked to tell people that I lived at the top of a castle. Spanish mission-style is how the real estate agent described it. Five apartments in the block, separated by an internal courtyard. Arched dormers, arcaded corridors, huge ceilings, chandeliers, articulated door surrounds.

'I hope I don't feel trapped inside a prison,' I'd said to the owner when I signed the lease.

She looked at me in horror. She was so proud of her renovations.

'The small windows,' I clarified. 'And no balcony.'

'Don't you want people to come and visit?' said Ingrid when I moved in to the top floor – seventy steps from street level.

'The steps aren't an issue for me. I guess I'm lucky.'

The windows were long slits in the wall that opened up on a view over the top of eucalyptus and Moreton Bay figs and across to Rose Bay.

A couple of months later, a psychic swung his crystal back and forth and said, 'It might be uncomfortable for a time but you need to move again. Somewhere closer to the ground.'

'You need to come down from your ivory tower,' was how Ingrid put it.

The sun shone on to the rolling freeways beside us as we walked – the bunkers, the smooth greens, the rising and falling terrain and the small contours. Water traps caused obstacles that were minor but challenging.

In my mind, I see my huge Victorian pine dresser and I've got an axe and I'm chopping the whole thing down. I could use it for firewood. But before I get to the dresser with the axe, I pull out the boxes and the folders and the files that I have neatly lined up in the colourful plastic sleeves and the cardboard boxes filled with the papers and more papers and photos and diaries and journals and every other damn thing I've saved and collected and stored. I'm imagining kicking the boxes after I drag them out of the dresser still covered with tiny dust particles from the drilling into the floor looking for concrete cancer in the place where I lived before last. I accidentally brought the dust with me to the new place – the place with the black-stained floors that still smell of the paint that they used for the renovation. I think that was the thing that made me cough in the night when I first moved in. I'm imagining getting rid of all that stuff that I've carted with me all these years and during all the moves and which I don't plan to take with me again – starting with the dresser that I used to love, that needs to be dismantled every time to fit through the doors. I'm sick of it all.

The noise of a leaf blower interrupted my thoughts. 'Whoever invented those things should be strung up in a public square and hung.'
Ingrid laughed.
On the golf course, a woman leaned forward pushing a golf trolley up the slope and behind her a man followed pulling his cart with one hand. He stopped for club selection and then the careful chip up the slope.
A red moped sped past with a young man and woman in shiny helmets, the woman's legs wrapped tightly around the man's thighs.

Ingrid and I completed the circumference of the golf course, leaving behind the weeping willow, the pepper tree, the melaleuca, the fig trees, the eucalypt, the red bottle brush and the cocos palm.

*

It is over. Absolutely over.

But I stand quite still, silent, or at most uttering a low moan, as I wait for the remembering to pass. This thinking about Vladimir is too distressing to be allowed to continue. It is like getting over a bad case of some debilitating virus. All energy is sucked out of me and the inertia descends.

I must move on.

He'd rung one Monday evening while I was boiling the kettle. I had just worked my way through the pile of bills next to the computer. I rushed to switch off the boiling water and answer the phone.

'Hello,' I said. 'Sofia here.'

'Sofia,' he said. 'How are you?'

'Hello, Vlad. What's happening?'

'Not much.'

'Any news on the work front?'

'No. The thing is, I don't want an office job where I have to sit at a desk all day.'

So nothing had changed.

'When will you know if you're free to make plans?' he said. 'When you're not too busy or too tired?'

I was surprised that he thought I wasn't free to see him. 'I can make plans.'

'Oh, really?'

'Do you want to do something on Saturday?'

'I can't plan ahead,' he said.

'Why not?' I was confused. Was he waiting to be asked over? It was early days in the relationship and I preferred to go out. Watching television wasn't my idea of a good time.

'It's only Monday,' he said. 'I don't know what I'm doing at the weekend.'

Why couldn't he make plans? He was only doing a little bit of translation work here and there. Plus dinner at his mother's three nights a week. He made some joke about her having ADD, something about her making demands on him for more attention, that she was never satisfied. I wondered if he thought of me in that way too – needy and demanding?

'Anything could happen before the weekend,' he said.

'Like what?'

'Like my friend Emily.'

I'd never met Emily but he talked about her a lot. Emily was in an on-again off-again relationship with a man she'd known only a couple of months. Every time it was off-again, Vladimir was there to pick up the pieces. They spoke on the telephone at least twice a day. I didn't like it.

'I don't know when Emily's getting back and I've arranged to pick her up from the airport. She might need a shoulder to cry on. I'm very busy helping my friends. That's the sort of person I am. I'll be busy for the next few weeks. Emily and I are very close. She and I are exactly the same.'

'The same? In what way?'

'I'm not going to tell you my secrets.'

'Just tell me one way in which you and she are the same.'

'We both fall in love very quickly.'

So who was he in love with?

'People throw the word love around so easily,' I snapped. 'It's lust, not love, when you've just met someone.' I heard the cynical tone in my voice and knew I sounded like some jaded woman-of-the-world.

A hum overhead reminded me to look up as a seaplane prepares to land on the bay, its belly exposed to the ocean. The shadow of a bird passed by on the other side of the glass.

'Emily sounds a bit silly to me,' I said. I couldn't stop myself from saying it.

'They're in love. I know exactly how she feels.'

'It's lust, not love.'

That's when he started in about the word love. 'Love is only a word,' he said. 'You must know there are many meanings of the word love. You must know that, as someone who likes to write poetry.'

'That's true.'

'You're looking at a tree. Right? Who said it's a tree?'

I didn't reply.

'Who?'

'You tell me.' So what was he trying to say?

'We agree it's a tree,' he said. 'It's the same with love. It's a word. What about obsession?'

'Yes, that's a better word,' I agreed. 'Obsession. We've all experienced that.' I knew all about the pain of obsession, but I hadn't thought I'd become enmeshed with someone like Vladimir.

'Are you and I obsessed with each other?' he asked.

'I'm not,' I said, far too quickly. 'I told you before, I need to take things slowly. But it would be nice to get together at the weekend.'

The knocking and banging sounds started up again from downstairs. The renovations that had been going on all year. I could hear Vladimir sigh above the noise.

'At our age it's about compromise,' he said. 'A lot of compromise. I believe that everything's negotiable. If people are willing.'

Thinking back now, I know that we were both struggling with the tricky business of intimacy – or lack of it.

Usually I like to walk early in the morning, when the earth is moist and the trees still silky with dew, when the sunlight filters between the long thin branches. But today I set off very late.

A postman hurries past. His long-sleeve fluoro-orange top flashes in the sunlight. The bulge of his stomach hangs over his belt as he puffs on a cigarette while plugged in to his iPod.

Perhaps I can remember things a little differently today.

There was that grey morning when I strode through the wooded area of the park and my thoughts were of nothing but Vladimir. I'd given him a call to see if he'd had the operation yet.

He hadn't. He was waiting for a place in the hospital but he was pleased I'd rung and suggested we get together. He could come over straight away. It was ages since I'd seen him, so I thought it would be a good opportunity to ask him why he hadn't returned my emails or calls. Why he'd cut off all communication.

When I opened the door to him, he greeted me with a long kiss and then hurried me into the bedroom. 'I'm so pleased you rang,' he said.

Later, when he was sitting in his underpants on the couch watching television, he explained why he hadn't been in touch. 'You said you didn't want to live with anyone.'

'Not straight away. Maybe after a while. After you've known someone for a long time.'

'You said you were a good cook. But you never invited me over for dinner.'

'I wouldn't say I was a good cook. I wouldn't say something like that.'

'You said you can cook, though.'

I made no reply.

Maybe Ingrid was right. The relationship with Vladimir never really began.

As I move deeper in among the trees, the bird sounds soften, become gentler, more mellow.

The wind picks up. It increases in intensity until it's like the roar of the ocean, swelling to a crescendo and then ebbing away, then building in intensity again. But I am warmed by the sun on my face and hands. Overhead are patches of brilliant blue as clouds drift across in a gentle glide. The wind builds again, behind me, in front of me. The gusts turn into a loud squall. The branches sway and twist in the wind like a forest of ballroom dancers. Gust after icy gust blows my hair around my face but the trees are constrained by their rigid postures.

I sit down under a gum tree, lean against it, feel its skin dig into my spine, then rest my head on its firm shoulder. It centres me this place. An insect flitters between the twigs. Green fronds in the centre of the trees, the outside fronds brown and dying – new shoots, old shoots, birth and death.

I get up, look around for my backpack, then sit down again, but under a different tree. Perhaps I can view things from another angle.

I'm remembering that day with Ingrid when we walked with her dog by the golf course. 'Did you ever see his place?' she'd asked. 'Did he ever ask you over? Did he ever take you out for dinner?'

'Of course not.'

Ingrid had sauntered ahead her ponytail swaying in the breeze.

I look around at the trees competing for light and try to take it all in. Whip birds whipping. Kookaburras laughing. It must be going to rain.

Jack

Alberto strides in through the door. We are waiting for him, all of us still rugged up in our coats, our dance bags on the chairs. He's been held up checking out a new venue for the dance on Saturday night. Alberto is a famous teacher of tango. He has a taut muscled body. He wears those special dance shoes that look like sneakers, but when he points his toes, the shoes flex almost in half. Several times a week, Alberto runs classes in different parts of Sydney, and once a month, he organises a social dance, also known as a milonga. I am very glad that I have found my way to Alberto's lessons, although it is not easy going back to beginner classes.

Recently my friend Nino said that Alberto has very high standards for his pupils, sometimes yelling at them, calling them 'hopeless' and 'stupid' because they keep making the same mistakes. Nino doesn't come to Alberto's classes any more. He is upset that some of the women think they are too good for him and step outside the circle when it is his turn to dance with them. I said to Nino that I intend to try different classes in order to find a regular dance partner for tango.

'I don't like to go to the dances in a hall,' Nino complained. 'A church hall or a community centre or a school or wherever. I like there to be a bar so I can have a few drinks when I dance. When I first split up with my wife, I went out to the Apia Club, where they had a band and dancing. I asked one woman to dance. She said no. I asked another woman to dance, she said no, so I went home and watched television. The next week, I went back to the Apia Club. I asked a woman to dance, she said no. I asked another woman to dance and she said no. I asked a third woman to dance. No. So I went home again and watched television. The next week, I went to the Concordia Club. I asked a woman to dance. No. Another woman. No. The third woman. Yes. We danced together and she said I danced quite well but could improve. She told me about the classes.'

Jack didn't dance at all.

I remember at a party when he took longer than I expected to come inside from smoking a cigarette and I decided he had met another woman. We'd been together a week, and I thought it was over already. The room seemed to empty of all sound and the people became lifeless. I couldn't hear the live band that I had been enjoying so much before. But then he came back and sat next to me on a soft stool on the floor and put his arms around me and we listened to the music of the band.

'Do you want to dance?' I asked.

'I don't dance,' he said.

'You just need to move to the music. Nothing complicated.'

He shook his head. 'I'm too self-conscious for that.'

The hall is at the back of a church on Oxford Street, Paddington. When I first started at Alberto's tango classes, I had trouble finding the entrance because it was hidden from the street. I was standing in a laneway, and it was only when I saw a man and a woman dressed in black entering a doorway that I knew I'd found the place.

The woman who arrived with Alberto is his dance partner and girlfriend. Or that's what Nino said. Nino said they turn up together at the milongas and leave together, so she must be his girlfriend.

On arrival at the hall, we all sat down to change into our dance shoes. The other women put on their strappy stiletto tango shoes that they've purchased in Argentina. I wear a pair of dance shoes from Bloch's with an ankle strap and a lower heel. I've had the podiatrist make a special arch support that replaces the original sole. He completely rebuilt the shoe so my body is more balanced and in alignment.

Tonight it's a small group in the class, all doing a double lesson. Beginners, then Intermediate, and all experienced dancers. Each week we start by practising alone, without a partner. First, the warm-up to stretch the legs and feet, the hip flexors and quads. We line up against the wall and stretch our calves and the backs of our legs. Then walking around the room – put your weight on one leg then move on to it – knees together with a slight bend, toe pointed and slightly turned out, stomach pulled up, shoulders down, toes and feet in constant contact with the floor. Balancing on one leg and then the other.

We partner up after practising alone, all in a line. As usual, there are not enough male partners, so the women pair up. Tonight I'm partnered with Susan: a tall angular woman. I sense her trying to take control when it's my turn to lead.

'I'll close my eyes,' she says. 'That will help me relax.'

The down lights in the ceiling heat the skin of our hands. There's the smell of dust on the slatted blinds at the windows.

We walk forward slowly, then backwards, up and down the room. Forward and backward ochos – step, swivel, step and swivel again.

'Make sure the shoulders stay to the front like they did against the wall,' Alberto instructs.

Alone and then with a partner we circle around a square on the floor to practise our giros. Both sides: left-side giro, then right-side giro. Open, step, swivel, step, open. One, two, three and four.

'Any questions at this point?' Alberto asks when the music stops.

'Do you touch the feet together on the "and" between three and four?' I ask.

'Yes,' he nods. 'Make sure that on the "and" before four, the feet touch lightly together.'

Many times I would drive along the main road out west following Jack's directions to pick him up. Along that road that curves around and under the pedestrian walkway and the park on the left. I'd turn right into his street and park under a tree opposite his lounge room window. From across the road, I would sense him sitting there waiting for me. Often he would appear outside with his backpack on his shoulder, ready to go with me in my car.

I stayed there only twice. The place had an awful smell that I'd noticed straight away. I couldn't identify it. Not mouldy, not cooking smells, just old smells. Smells that seemed to indicate that a lot of unpleasant things had happened there. I didn't know then that it was a halfway house. One thing I did know, because I'd asked him directly, was that there had been only a few other women, but each of them had left him.

'I'm not easy,' he said when we broke up the first time. 'No one finds me easy.'

We're practising walking the length of the hall. Alberto says that in Buenos Aires students of tango spend two years just learning to walk properly.

'Extend forward,' he says, 'step forward, only placing the weight on the extended leg at the last moment, toes pointed, sides of the feet staying connected to the floor.'

Then backwards with a straight leg, torso pulled up, chest up and out – and with a partner again, always there's that special connection with a partner.

'Try and choose someone the same height,' he says.

This time I'm partnered with a young Asian woman named Nancy. She's a tiny-framed woman and we are the same height – perfect for tango. I can smell the brightness of the washing powder on her clothes as she moves in close to me.

'Feel the connection but stay grounded, not forcing,' says Alberto. 'A conversation between two bodies to the music,' he enthuses. 'Feel the music. Really feel the music while connecting with a partner.'

By the side of the room are the dance bags and the street shoes lined up under the chairs. The ceiling fan spins above our heads. You can almost feel the chill of its steel blades, our eyes dry in their sockets.

And then the adornments. First by ourselves and then together. One toe tracing a circle on the floor. Both feet parallel as one foot goes around, out from the big toe with a circle.

'Circle, circle then step to the side.' Alberto demonstrates. His feet look like those of a ballerina even though they are encased in thick rubber.

We practise in a line behind him.

'The circle should go no farther forward than the big toe,' he says, his foot very delicately pointed, the arch clearly defined. 'You can choose to have the knee up and trace the circle with a pointed foot, or have a flatter foot, which makes a thicker circle. The women can use the heel of their shoes rather than their toes to trace it.'

The fan is reflected in the two mirrors, one mirror directly opposite the other. Ceiling fans in mirrors – on and on – into infinity.

'Find something to put on the floor that is the shape of a square,' instructs Alberto.

I take the *Sydney Morning Herald* out of my handbag and fold it in half. Other people find pieces of paper or even their street shoes to use as a marker. Nancy and I square up and then we begin. We circle the square on the floor, making sure to keep our shoulders parallel to each other. We take turns being the person who decides it's time for a change of direction from left side giro to right side giro. Who will lead and who will follow?

The women at tango aren't very friendly. Well, two are, two aren't. One was, but isn't any more. That first week, when we'd been partnered for one of the exercises, Susan had seemed quite nice. We'd walked to our cars together after the lesson and she'd asked if I was coming to the dance on Saturday night. But some of the women are such bitches. Like Cynthia and Rosemary and Tina and the other aggressive women who come up and take a man right out from under your nose. You'll be having a conversation, about to dance together and they come up without even waiting for a pause and ask the man to dance.

I have only one photograph of Jack, taken at a fancy dress party. In this photo his hair and eyebrows are dyed bright red, so it is not a picture I like to show people.

'You mightn't recognise me,' he'd said on the phone that first time. 'I'll be wearing a jacket and tie.'

But there he was sitting up towards the back of the beer garden keeping warm under one of those metal flame heaters. I kissed him hello and inhaled peppermint, hair shampoo and cigarettes.

'I'm just sucking a breath freshener,' he said as I sat down beside him. Then he put his hand on mine. 'I've only got ten dollars on me,' he said with a look of childlike defiance, as if he expected me to challenge him. 'It's best to say it up front.'

So he only had ten dollars. That was okay. Enough for a glass of wine. And that's all I was there for. A quick drink and then I'd go home.

'What do you want?' he asked. 'Wine? I need a drink when I'm with a woman.'

So he too was nervous.

'Don't worry,' I said standing up. 'I'll get it.'

I pulled my cardigan down at the back, feeling self-conscious. He was probably watching me from behind when I walked to the bar.

When we clinked glasses, he said how nice it was to see me again, that our paths had crossed once more.

His thick eyebrows shadowed his face. 'You look nice,' he said. 'I like your necklace.'

I fingered the tiny terracotta and silver beads threaded in rows close to my neck. Velvet cord jeans, camel cardigan, high-heeled boots, chocolate wool jacket. He asked if I still live by the water. We talked about the old days in the film industry and the people we'd known and who we'd stayed in touch with and what these people were doing now. Which ones had been able to keep working in the business.

'The ones who've survived financially are the ones who've had help from their partners or from their families,' he said with envy in his tone.

He wanted to show me his pilot program on the computer that was in his backpack on the floor. 'Let's go back to your place and watch it,' he said. 'Let's get another bottle and take it with us. I'll pay you back.'

Tonight I sit in this huge empty space. Hollow footsteps at the end of the day. A glimpse of green through glass. The rain that has been hovering all afternoon fills the gutters and pours down the drainpipes and makes the leaves on the trees bend down from the weight of it all. The breeze feels cool through the flyscreens. The phone rings. It's Alberto to say the milonga will be at the Crystal Ballroom on Saturday night.

'What do you think will be the proportion of men to women?' I ask.

'More men.'

'I don't want to sit like a wallflower. It's bad for my self-esteem.'

'Don't worry. I'll dance with you. I'll dance with you so much that you'll be too tired to dance with anyone else.'

I laugh when he says that. It really makes me laugh.

Jack had held my hand as we walked to the car that first night. The side of the road was brightly lit by street lights and floodlights around the hotel. The other side of the road was dark, lined with trees that shaded the road from the electric lights. Power lines intersected between the leaves. I asked him to drive. He strapped himself in to the driver's seat after first handing me the seat belt. He waited until I clicked myself in.

At my place, we settled back on the couch and watched his video. It was an introduction to a series he wanted to produce. Just a piece to camera, that was all. His arm was along the back of the couch behind me. Beyond our reflection in the window, a storm approached from the east. There was the thud of thunder. The horizon seemed dulled and dampened – white waves looked fluorescent against the dark sea.

'How old are you?' he asked.

'You know how old my kids are, so you can guess.'

'You're not that much older than me.'

'A fair bit older. Fourteen years.'

I got up then and pulled back the sliding door and went out onto the balcony, where the air was thick with the smell of the sea. He followed me out and moved up behind and nestled his face into the back of my neck. I held onto the terrace as he pressed against me, felt the force of him from behind, the coolness of the steel railing against my stomach. He kissed my hair, the side of my neck, and I leant back into him. The wind whistled up the gully. The sound of distant thunder. His mouth was soft, gently probing with his tongue. A flash of lightning out to sea. Thunder, louder this time, cracked the sky.

We moved into the bedroom. I worried about the brightness of the light next to the bed near my face. His fingers were in the loops of my clothes. He didn't bother undressing. The sweet moist smell of rain. Another flash of lightning. The thunder claps louder and deeper and broader in spectrum. His eyes were closed. The rain gathered momentum. Pounded the railing of the balcony. It kept on. Constant and relentless.

It was good.

Sleeping is always difficult. I can't sleep because I'm thinking – nothing productive. I fall asleep only after I have persuaded myself that tomorrow will reveal the answer.

In the picture I have of him in my mind, I see his flawless skin, inhale the moistness of it, but see again his stained teeth, his shoulders drooped forward. He is dressed in cargo pants with sections at the side. There are holes in his trousers and his small change falls through and leaves a trail of silver. We noticed the coins once when we walked back down the stairs after visiting some friends of mine. He said his post office box key caused the perforations. I sewed the tear up. 'No one has ever done that for me before,' he said. Some time later, he told me that one of the holes had returned and that he was still putting his sharp little key in his pocket.

This morning, when all the shadows of the long night had faded, I opened the glass sliding doors and walked out on to the balcony. In the gully a solitary white-bellied sea-eagle was waltzing with the wind. I watched as head-over-heels he plunged before adjusting his centre of balance and, with wings outstretched, realigned himself into a glide.

Tango

Just before nine o'clock in the evening, Sofia gets out of her car and looks up at the sky. She has sensed a shift in the weather. There is another breath of wind, a whispering in the air, but the clouds are stagnant against the dark night. She turns and moves downhill towards the ballroom, ejecting the chewing gum from her mouth with a loud splat into the bushes, feels the first drops of rain on her bare arms. She passes the public phone box where frangipanis lie on the grass, picks one up, sniffs at it, throws it back, then quickly enters the building.

It is not one of her best days. She doesn't know why. Her dress is not uncomfortable, her skirt just right around the waist, the outfit not faded or pilled, her black strappy shoes high, not too high, wrapped around her feet following the shape of her instep, and the new shampoo and conditioner make her hair curl naturally around her face. For reassurance, she strokes the pearl and bronze necklace nestled into the groove of her neck.

At reception, she pauses to flash her card and takes the lift to the third floor and then continues along the long hall, at the end of which is the thud and bounce of Latin American dance music.

She turns into the room, which is set up with tables and chairs in a horseshoe shape around the wooden dance floor, the dee jay on the stage above and a bar at the back of the room. She sees Nino down the front sitting with that older couple he usually sits with and wonders whether or not to join them.

'Sofia, you'll never find a rich husband if you're fat,' said Mother, raising her glass. It was Mother's fifty-third birthday. Her hair was silvery with flecks of white now that she'd let her own natural colour grow through.

'How would you know?' Sofia's older brother said, picking his nose and flicking the snot across the table at his mother.

Everyone said he was a radical, that boy. He did things a certain way. But somehow they still thought the sun shone out of his arse. Everyone laughed. The entire family – even the aunt and uncle and the two boy cousins – drinking the kosher wine at the seder table. The moment passed.

Alone in her room, Sofia sang along with the radio station, volume turned way up. 'The Happy Wanderer'. 'I love to go a wandering along the mountain track, and as I go I love to sing, my knapsack on my back.'

She would practise her leaps across the room in front of the mirror. See how far she could cross in one amazing jump, her back leg extended behind her as she leapt into the air from a running start.

She dances with Nino at the Crystal Ballroom every Friday night. Now that Nino is semi-retired, he dances four nights a week, plays tennis and works out at the gym when he's not working part-time as an accountant. He has grey hair combed back from a high forehead and around his neck is a brown leather thong with a small silver medallion. The leather thong makes him look more attractive, more unusual, more interesting. He likes to show the younger women how to dance.

The tall Portuguese man with the dyed black hair (she assumes it's dyed), described Nino as a vampire. But then he is probably jealous of the number of different women that Nino is able to get to join him at his table.

Jordan, the taxi driver, who dances to keep his weight down, said that Nino only likes to dance the tango so he can feel the women's breasts pressed against him.

'He didn't say that,' said Sofia in disbelief. 'Nino is a gentleman, he wouldn't say that.'

Jordan was ready to wave Nino over to confirm the story.

Sometimes Sofia sits by herself with her coat on the chair beside her, pretending she is here with a friend, and the friend is on the dance floor and that's why she's sitting there alone.

Sofia is working on a book of family history. Things have changed very much, several times since she grew up, and like everyone in Sydney, she has led several lives and she still leads some of them. Since she started the book, she has gone out with two South American tango dancers, one Irish dance teacher, and a revolutionary playwright who patted her thigh and said, 'Where is this relationship going? I would like it to be more. My wife isn't interested in sex any more.'

Her children are grown-up and lead their own lives. Sometimes the sheer unpredictability, the randomness of the way she is living, what she is doing, fills her with exhilaration.

For the past six months, she has been seeing a man from Leichardt. As far as she can see, this is over. She calls him J, as if he were a character in a novel that pretends to be true.

J is the first letter of his name, but she chose it also because it seems to suit him. The letter J seems to give a promise of youth and vitality. It is upright and strong, with very straight vertebrae. And using just the letter, not needing a name, is in line with a system she often employs these days. She says to herself, France, 1993, and she sees a whole succession of scenes, the apricots and salmons of the buildings and the turquoise of the Mediterranean Sea.

Dressed for salsa? said the counsellor with a grin as he closed the door behind her.

I don't remember telling you that I danced salsa, she said as he extracted her file from the drawer of the metal filing cabinet. I think you're getting me confused with someone else.

In O'Connell Street or Liverpool Street. I can picture it.

I used to dance at Glebe Town Hall on Sunday nights, but that was ages ago.

Your salsa phase, he confirmed. He moved from the filing cabinet to the large grey seat opposite her. Any stallions beating at your door? he said with a note of expectancy in his voice.

They're all pathetic. It's hopeless.

He gasped in a pretending way.

Not all of them, she corrected herself. Just the ones I engage with.

He wrote that down.

It's all over with the Fireman, she volunteered. He's married anyway.

You can cross Fireman off the list now.

I've been through the list. It's been so many years. I've met one of everything.

He said with a smirk, Of course. Zookeeper.

She shrugged, remembering the organic gardener. I've probably met one of those too.

The last time she saw J, or rather what she thought would be the last time, she was standing at the turnstiles at Town Hall station and he came through the gate sweating, his face and body flushed, his hair damp.

It was a hot night in September. They'd had a meal together at a Spanish restaurant in the city. She remembers how flushed his skin was, but has to imagine his boots, his broad white thighs as he crouched or sat, and the open friendly expression he must have worn on his face, talking to her, she, who wanted nothing from him any more. She knows she was conscious of how she looked standing there under the neon light, and that in this glare she might seem even older to him than she was, and also that he might find her less attractive.

He went to get a cup of coffee, then came back out. He stood beside her and looked down with his arm almost around her. She sensed his hesitation to touch her. She kissed him on the cheek and he looked deep into her eyes and she knew what he wanted her to say. Saw the pleading expression he must have worn on his face.

Have you lost weight? she asks Dan, one of her regular dance partners as she flicks her foot back and behind his knee into a gancho. The movement is like a horse trying to shake its shoe from its hoof.

Make sure your heel is up when you do the gancho, Alfred had told her. Sweep your leg along the floor and out. Not up with the leg, but up with the heel.

She reminds herself to make sure her shoulders are down. Firm arms, shoulders down. She's sure that's why she gets so much neck pain.

Alfred, bald, shiny-headed Alfred, who Nino says looks like a gangster with his shaved head and black T-shirt, still thinks everyone on the dance floor sets out to block his movement around the room. There's no doubt about him. At least he started out friendly enough.

Dan smells good for a change and he's lost his big stomach that used to come between them. Sometimes she would gag with the smell of him.

Yes, he says as they bounce lightly to the beat of a milonga. I got sick with the flu for a couple of weeks last year and decided to keep the weight off.

During a break in the sets, she sits down next to Alfred.

What do I look like? Alfred says, inclining his head towards the dance floor. I wish I knew what I looked like.

I don't know, she says. I wasn't watching you.

He sighs with disappointment.

And he's made up a step. She must tell him she doesn't want to do his stupid made-up step, which is a cross with her left leg, but when she feels his opposite hip against hers she doesn't know if it's a gancho or not. But the main problem, which she must tell him, is that he pulls her off her axis, her centre.

Would you do it if it wasn't made up? he says now they're up and dancing a vals.

It's not that I won't do it, she says. I can't do it. I'm not deliberately not doing it, she says, unable to disguise her anger. Should she make a scene and leave the dance floor and leave him standing there because he's being so rude and aggressive because she can't do his stupid made-up step?

Do you speak to the other women like you speak to me?' she says, not caring who can hear.

I can't understand why you won't do it.

I can't do it.

I wish I knew what that little voice was saying in your head. His hip pushes hard into her, very hard, so she is forced into the backward lock from the left leg.

Wheep wheep, wheep wheep, wheep wheep went the big shiny knife against the hard grey stone. Father would carve the roast lamb each week for the Sunday lunch. After lunch they'd go to the hospital to visit Grandpa. Grandpa without his left leg, then without his right leg. Gangrene. He passed away piece by piece.

Left foot, left leg. Right foot, right leg.

The women at the dances look beautiful in a cruel way, with their blood-red lips and their nails long and sharp. They are not very friendly. Sofia is just a casual, after all. She hasn't signed up for a ten-week course and she doesn't go to the beginners lesson at seven-thirty.

Things have not changed very much on the dance scene since she started there so many years ago. 'Same old, same old,' as she heard the Turkish woman describe the previous Saturday's dance at Marrickville to the Egyptian woman with the red red lips.

What a beautiful smile you have, said the woman on the door who takes the money. Did anyone tell you that your whole face smiles when you smile?

She's nice. She's the partner of the man who runs the dance. She says she doesn't mind that she doesn't get to dance on the Friday nights because she dances nearly every other night of the week at the lessons. She's very beautiful. Russian with long blonde hair against her tanned smooth olive skin, very long shiny legs and always one of her very short cut up the side skirts that she makes herself. She's Sofia's age.

When Father came back from the factory in the evenings, the children, pale and silent, joined him for his dinner. After dinner, Father listened to the radio in the lounge with his newspaper, and at seven Mother, having washed up, joined him. The family were together only at dinner, after which Mother and Father sat behind their newspapers and the children went upstairs to their rooms. Sometimes a stupid child would pull the wings off a fly or even a butterfly and watch it suffer.

A new man makes his way around the dance floor. Good posture. Straight back, strong arm position. Looks like he'd be a good strong lead. The music stops and he comes over and sits on the spare seat beside Sofia.

'It's all too heat-making for an old man like me,' he jokes as he fans himself furiously with a bingo brochure. 'I'm a postman from Perth on holiday in Sydney,' he says by way of an introduction in a well-modulated English voice. 'I could have had a two-week holiday in Paris for the price of this three-day trip to Sydney.'

She smiles. 'Have you read *The Post Office* by Charles Bukowski?'

'We're not very cultural in Perth.'

'You speak very well for a postman.'

'Well,' he shrugs, as if that is a whole other story that he will not go into at this stage, 'dancing the tango allows me to meet famous people all over the world,' he says. 'In Paris, London, New York. My name is Fabian by the way.'

'That's a very romantic name. I grew up in the era of Fabian the pop star.'

'In Perth we all live in one big waiting room,' he adds. 'We're all waiting. Not much culture or adventure. There are many French and Italian speaking women who dress like the women you see in Paris. The tango community is very close. If one person learns a new step, then everyone learns it. Two weeks later, we're all doing it.'

'You've lost weight,' the doctor said when she'd walked in.

She shrugged. 'It's wonderful what black does. Just one item of black.'

He looked down at his shoes with the regular pattern of holes punched towards the pointed toes. 'What about black shoes?' he asked.

'Your feet look smaller,' she reassured him.

'You know what they say about small feet,' he laughed.

She assumed he meant small feet, small penis. She sat down opposite him, a box of tissues between them on the small square table. 'It's hands,' she says. 'Not feet. Fingers.'

He uncapped his pen, looked down at his notes.

'You're not going to start on that track already, are you?' she said. 'Not so early in the session.'

I grew up dancing the polka in Italy, says Nino as they turn into a Viennese waltz.

How was your holiday? she asks.

Very boring.

Didn't you play tennis with your grandsons?

He pulls a face. Did you meet any nice European men while you were away? he asks.

I was married to an Austrian. From Vienna.

Did you see him there?

He lives in Sydney.

She says this simply to establish that she had a husband once, that she had been married, and to a European man, an interesting man, a man of cultural heritage. She wants to assure Nino that she was not always alone, unattached.

Does Anthony ask you to dance? Nino asks.

No. He doesn't.

He should.

There are no shoulds. I asked him once and he went off across the floor doing his own thing. It was very humiliating.

Nino nods and grins with no understanding in his demeanour.

Anthony has many choices, he says, as if that would explain it. He's young and he's a good dancer. A lot of the women are after him.

She remembers Mother saying to her when she was a teenager, 'It's a man's world.' But Mother had two children by the time she was seventeen.

Sofia's daughter likes to paint. Sometimes Sofia minds Kate's two children while Kate goes to a lesson. This afternoon she was over at Kate's house looking after the baby and the two-year-old.

'I feel like Superman when I mind the kids and then go out tango dancing,' Sofia likes to tell her friends. 'At three o'clock, I'm on the oval kicking a football around with my grandson and then at seven-thirty I'm changing into my tight skirt with a split up the side and my red top and my strappy high-heeled shoes and I'm out the door again. Like Clark Kent changing into his Superman cape.'

Have you got a dance partner? her friends, or maybe her brother, might ask.

Various, she'll say. I've got various. Several.

Today when Kate got back, Sofia told her she'd brought the washing in because it had started to sprinkle with rain.

Was it dry?

I think so.

You think so?

Well, I was rushing to bring it in before it poured with rain and I had two children to look after at the same time and the baby was awake and the noise of the builders next door and the electrician with his ladder and his cords everywhere and I couldn't even get to the toilet.

Well, when you brought the washing in, did you do all the ironing? Kate asked her mother. Did you iron all the clothes when you brought them in?

They both laughed. It was a joke.

Sofia doesn't really own a tight skirt with a split up the side, but she wishes she did have one. And nice long legs to show off. Instead, she usually wears the same pair of black trousers that she hopes will slim her down, and one of her many pretty tops. Well, actually, that's not true either. She wears the same black camisole top, or one of the two similar black camisole tops, and a sheer cardigan on the top to disguise, to cover, to conceal, to pretend, that her arms aren't so fat, that her freckled skin doesn't look so blotchy in the light. But usually it gets so hot she has to strip down to the black pants and the black camisole top with her hair pulled high on top of her head so it doesn't hang in wet cat's tails around her face.

'I think the baby looks like me,' Sofia said to Kate as she reached for the old brown photo album. 'Have a look,' she said pointing to a photograph of herself in Class 8. 'Here I am. Can you see me?'

'Oh, yes.'

'I'm the one on the end. The little Miss Perfect sitting up so straight.'

'You do look different to the others.'

'I'm the one trying too hard.'

'You're the only one wearing a tie.'

'Can we get a photocopy of her?' Alfred says as Jordan comes over and leads her towards the dance floor.

Jordan's style is firm and masculine. She likes the smell of the mint that he always sucks or chews.

After a good half hour of dancing in the hot auditorium, he speaks. 'If they have a Latin bracket,' he says. 'Will you dance it with me?'

Afterwards they sit back at Nino's table with the much older couple.

'You and Jordan dance well together,' says the man so stiff with arthritis it takes him a long time to stand up, to unwrap his legs and put his whole weight on his feet. But he does. He gets up each week to dance with his lady friend and they shuffle around over in a dark corner after a couple of glasses of white wine and they are into their second packet of potato chips.

'You look like you should be married,' the older man continues. 'Like you should have babies together.'

'Who? Me and Jordan?' Sofia says, trying to sound casual about the possibility of her and Jordan. She quite likes Jordan. But only because he dances salsa and rumba and rock and roll so well. He smells nice, he dances well, what more could she want? But of course Jordan has a regular girlfriend, but the girlfriend doesn't come to the Friday night dances.

Jordan laughs. 'She's a grandmother already,' he says with a dismissive flick of his hand towards Sofia. 'We couldn't have children together.'

'Here's a photo of Grandpa and me. I'm standing beside his wheelchair. It's a black and white photo that shows him only from just above the knees, which is where the rug would have ended that covers his lap. I look about thirteen in this picture. My tall gawky stage. Long hair pulled back severely, a cardigan to hide my developing breasts. Mother hated my hair. I think she must have spent her whole life telling me how dreadful my hair looked. I'm smiling in the photo and leaning down to put my face a little bit closer to Grandpa.'

Outside, a bird chimed in a cheerful tone and the leaves of the jacaranda tree whispered in the wind. The beautiful jacaranda tree. They had one like that once. She thought she'd miss that tree and that house but although she did at first, after a while she came to love the different place where she moved to. And then this place where she lives now, by the sea, the place where J came to live with her. The place where they pretended they could live together. Where he went off to work every day and she kissed him goodbye at the front door. The place where he'd come home to her at night.

'I'll fill in a form for you to have a blood test whenever you want. You won't have to come and see me first. You can go straight there.' He walks over to his desk. 'Anything else you want tested?'

'You'd better add iron. And the test for blood sugar. A family history of diabetes.'

'Those arms look like they've done a lot of work,' said the nurse as she tightened the strap around Sofia's arm.

'What do you mean? How can you tell?'

'The veins. You've got good veins. The veins are connected to the muscles.'

When she was a teenager, she'd wanted to have dance lessons. 'I learnt to dance without lessons,' Mother had said. 'So you can too.'

There were huge waves out to sea after the winds of the night. The biggest she'd ever seen, in fact. They really were magnificent. She'd listened to the winds as they'd thrashed the ocean waves through the branches of the trees.

'Step further across for the forwards ochos,' said the visiting Argentinian dance teacher. 'Step further back behind me for the turn and swivel. Keep your left hip down when doing a forwards ocho. Caress the floor with your feet. No feet in the air. Relax your right shoulder. Keep your shoulders down. Do the cross whether the man leads you into it or not.' (She thinks that's what he said.) 'Be heavy on the front foot in the cross. Weight forwards. Keep your knees together when you do an adornment. Keep the adornments simple. Just do one or two. Polish the leg and then down again; then step over. Slow down on the turns. Don't run. Keep your right wrist firm. In the open embrace, let your arms go up and down the man's arm. Up to behind his neck and then down to his forearm.'

'You've had a lesson with the best,' said Pedro.

'I've been saving myself,' she'd said proudly.

It was about six-thirty on a Friday. Early summer. The bougainvilleas and the jacarandas were already in bloom but no frangipanis yet. She'd been waiting for J to come home, looking forward to his return from the city, hoping they'd sit together with a drink outside on the balcony. He'd have a shower and get changed and then they'd go out for the meal that he'd promised her.

Instead he was on the phone, his face slightly in shadow but well lit enough for her to see the ever-present cigarette. Half inside, half outside so he could exhale out the door. His voice droned on and on. The wind increased in force. A strong wind, blowing against her head, her hair, her hands. Her furious heart beat hard against the walls of her ribs. Then the wind died down again and she could only hear his voice; not the sound of the birds any more or the movement of the leaves on the trees.

It rained a lot that night. The sound of the waterfall below. The sound of water after rain.

It's all your fault anyway, she said to the counsellor.

He looked puzzled.

You said to me, 'It's your body. You can do what you like with it,' in that moralising tone of yours.

I would have only said that, he said gently, if I thought you were being too generous with your body.

After that bit of moralising, I've turned that whole side of myself off. Anyway, I have no libido. So it's not such an issue any more.

Well, that's good. He took a sip of his coffee that surely must be cold already. There's more to me than you think, he said.

You're very blinkered, she said. She held up her hands beside her face to imitate a horse with covers at the side of his eyes. Straight. You haven't got an open mind. In some areas, she clarified.

He pulled a face.

I bet your daughter, or daughters, tell you that.

They're too polite, he said.

Your daughter looked lovely by the way. The one I saw last time.

The blonde?

Yes. I thought you had a son and a daughter.

No. I've got three daughters.

Three daughters? And a son?

Yes. So you think I need to open my chakras? he joked.

She shrugged. Chakras spin, they don't open.

You might be surprised. I could be a Buddhist.

Is my time up? she said with an anxious glance at the clock.

It's okay, he reassured her. I hadn't noticed.

At dusk, the last of the brightness of the pink sighed above the horizon.

The sea a woolly blanket of blue and white. The same four palm trees all in a row between the road and the beach. The pale face of the moon two-thirds of the way to the sky. One-eighth of the side of its face missing but still the moon looked down, almost expressionless. A woman flashed the blue of her helmet as she cycled with strong thighs up Bronte Road, head bent in concentration on the road ahead as a bus bellowed black dust. The pink of the sky turned into mauve mixed with blue as the French cook arrived with his pale blue scarf knotted like a boy scout tight around his neck. With his right hand he checked his balls for reassurance as he mounted the step into the café.

It is unusual for Sofia to be outside these days, but no more odd than spending hours inside at the Mitchell Library looking at microfilm or walking through Waverley Cemetery looking for graves, no more odd than her work, or the people stuck on hot trains and buses trying to get home from work, or other places where people find themselves as they struggle to get through their days.

Times change, your life changes and you need to shift.

At our age, we're not going to improve our game of tennis, said the man on Bare Island.

Speak for yourself, she'd said.

The brown bird with a black triangle on his head jumped on the green see saw of a branch. Up and down he went, up and down, until he flew off again in a southerly direction.

'The bastards,' the counsellor said as a joke, with a tilt of his head and a puffing out his cheeks as if he was about to spit on the ground in disgust.

'I love it when you do that,' she laughed. 'That's the way it is exactly.'

Back home after the dance, she'd gone straight to her room. She'd turned on the lamp and knelt on the bed to pile the cushions up. Tears came almost to her eyes, her stomach empty with sadness. It was all such a bloody fantasy. She stared around at the night silence, then huddled in her bed.

She had a box of a hundred Dilmah tea bags that she'd bought especially for J. When the box is empty, she told herself, the pain will have eased.

Six months later, she walked outside to the balcony, sat on the chaise longue that they'd chosen together and looked down the gully at the grey sea. She drank the last tea bag from the box.

The tea was strong and hot, and so bitter it parched her tongue.

Hanif

'So Jack was the big love?' says Ingrid.

Sofia shrugs and looks out the window to the pavement outside the café, hears the swish of cars on the wet road like water pouring into a washing machine, the sound coming through the conversations all around them and the clattering of plates from the kitchen.

'Which one was Jack?' Ingrid persists. 'Did I ever meet him?'

'No, you didn't meet him. And you didn't meet Hanif either.'

Ingrid had spotted me at the café by the harbour this very cool and wet morning, where all the windows are closed and the air is speckled with light rain. It's the size of her hair that always first catches one's attention. A small head with a helmet of teased and lacquered blonde hair. She stood outside the window under the awning, where water dripped over the canvas, talking to a man, in that way she has, at once interested and encouraging, motionless and at attention like a soldier.

'Was Hanif good-looking?' she wants to know when she's seated across the table from me and I tell her that I had a coffee with a new bloke.

'Yes. Very handsome.'

The thing is, it's not easy being the one who does all the telling. It seems that in relationships with friends, sometimes there's one who does all the asking and the other who feels an obligation to do most of the telling.

'It's a control thing,' said our mutual friend Amanda, when I was having a whine about the fact that Ingrid and I seem to have run out of things to talk about. Amanda had asked if Ingrid and I still met every week for a coffee.

'We didn't meet last week. She didn't ring me and I didn't ring her. Lately we seem to have run out of things to say, unless I'm telling her some long story.'

'Maybe she doesn't say much about herself because she doesn't want to show her vulnerability,' said Amanda.

'Sometimes we end up sitting there in silence. I ask her about her work and her family and this and that and whether she and Dennis have been out dancing recently, then can't think of anything else to say. The way she asks me questions is invasive, but recently there doesn't seem much we've got to say to each other. She doesn't offer any information.'

'Maybe she's got problems at home.'

'Perhaps. Last time she had problems with Dennis she didn't want to talk about it. "Too personal," she said. She doesn't want to tell me her intimate stuff but expects me to tell her.'

Then Amanda mentioned she'd seen Ingrid in the change room at the gym recently. 'For someone who does so much exercise, she doesn't have a great body.'

'I think she gets stuck into the biscuits at night. They don't go out much any more, she and Dennis. He prefers to sit at home watching Foxtel. But then he falls asleep in front of the telly and wakes up at the end of the movie and asks what it was all about.'

'That wouldn't be much fun. Do they still go out dancing?'

'Very occasionally. It's a shame. You'd think that would be the perfect relationship. A guy who dances.'

It was the Saturday morning of the long weekend that Hanif walked along the path to the café. I hurried along to meet him, my hands deep in my wool coat. He hadn't seen me yet. I knew it was probably him because I could see his black hair and I noticed the well-tailored look of his clothing. Not the usual gear you'd wear to the beach.

My hands were icy cold and clammy at the same time and there was the taste of anxiety in my mouth. I clutched the gloves in the pockets of my coat.

His grey cotton shirt hugged his toned body, but hung loose over the top of his tight black jeans. There was a boyishness in his stature

– slim and taut. I said I'd known it was him when I saw him below on the path.

'I recognised you straight away,' he said. He nodded at my backpack. Been walking?

'No. I just like to walk around the long way into this park.'

'I've been here to swim but I didn't know there was a café.' He smiled with a broad grin. 'You look like your photo. Not like some people.'

We hovered there at the bottom of the steps where the tables and chairs were set up outside. Did I want to sit inside or out? He liked to be in the sun.

'Sure. We can sit outside but I'll keep my back to the sun.'

'Is this where you go in to order?' he said, looking up to the glass doors. He'd go and find out. I could choose where to sit.

The tables were beginning to turn gold in the sun that arched slowly above the Moreton Bay figs; the dry faded wood seemed to glow with life.

Hanif sat opposite me to begin the introductions. 'I've kissed a lot of frogs is what women say. It's the same for me. But what is it that a man should say?'

I shrugged and watched as the waitress in black sheer stockings, knee-high boots and short dress placed the coffees on the table with a thud. The flounces on the hem of her dress flicked up in the breeze that blew across from the water. It was a relief he wasn't watching her. I noticed the freshly applied red lipstick and the large open pores of her face that were covered with thick make-up. What would Hanif think now he could see me in the harsh sunlight? The tinny taste of caffeine was on my milk-fuzzed tongue as I worried about my own imperfections.

He leant back on his chair, stretched his legs and puffed his chest out with a sigh before telling me a little about his life back in Persia and his business that went bankrupt. 'Retail is tough. Very tough.' He savoured the chocolate topping from his coffee, the cup in the palm of his hands, like a delicate bird's nest.

A myna bird hopped on to the table beside us and jerked his head from side to side, up down and around. He pecked at the crumbs of food left between the slatted wood of the table top before flying off without a second thought. Free. Free as a bird. Able to take off at a whim.

Hanif's eyes rested on my lips when I spoke, his mouth tight with concentration. Then he stood up and resettled himself beside me. 'So your shadow doesn't hide me,' he said with a grin that revealed his even white teeth.

I knew he might reach for my hand. The winter morning wind felt cold against the back of my neck as my hair blew wildly around my face.

He reached out his hand to cover mine. The paleness of his fingernails looked almost white against the darkness of his skin. I allowed him to turn my hand over and to feel the sensitive flesh of my palm.

'Soft skin,' he said. 'Lovely hair.'

He raised his eyes until I could see his face through the black fringe of hair that fell across it. His brown eyes shimmered, all shiny and bright, but dark and clear at the same time. It was confusing; he seemed to be able to look all the way into my heart. I buttoned my woollen jacket up closer to my throat.

'Are your shoes suitable for a walk on the beach?' he asked with a broad smile.

He seems as trusting as a puppy, I thought.

The black leather toes of my boots were covered with sand.

'Look! Is that a hoof mark?' he said. 'Are there horses on the beach?'

'A horse on the beach?'

'Or someone wearing boots,' he laughed.

I put my hand in my pocket so he couldn't hold it. Could anyone see me? It was a mistake to have chosen this harbour beach so close to where I live. Would I look ridiculous holding hands with someone so young. Who was I trying to fool?

'Where do you go to dance?' I asked.

After all, that's why I was there. I wanted a new dance partner. He'd written that he'd learnt salsa and tango. At least he had the posture of a dancer, standing tall, shoulders back, chest proud. He'd be able to lead with his upper body in the Argentine tango.

'I went to a milonga last night at the Rocks,' he said. 'But I get so jealous of those South American men. The ones with the ponytails. They're so confident and they look so good on the floor. They can dance with anyone they like.'

'I could meet up with you at a dance,' I said.

'I'm not very good.'

'That's okay. I just want to get out of the house and back on the dance floor.'

'You can invite me to a dance.'

Not what I had in mind. Why did I have to be the one to do the asking?

A man launched a sea kayak into the water in front of us as Hanif spoke a little about his last girlfriend. He said the sex was great. 'She'd had a boob job, though. You'd be feeling the warmth of her body and then get to her breasts – they were cool. No life in them. You haven't had a boob job, have you?'

I shook my head. We were nearing the end of the beach where the big rocks would block our path. We wouldn't be able to walk any further.

'Where are you taking me?' he joked.

'Nowhere.' Absolutely nowhere.

We strolled back along the path that led through the trees of the park. When we got to my car, he manoeuvred us into a position where he could wrap both arms around me and kiss me on the mouth. There in broad daylight in the suburbs. It made me want to laugh at the silliness of it all. Then he lifted me up into the air, backpack and all, and let me slide back down the front of his body.

'You're so strong,' I said.

And then he was hugging me close again and wanting me to place my hand on the bulge in his trousers.

I moved away. Ingrid would have slapped him across the face.

'You can give me a lift to my car,' he said.

'I'm not doing that. You'll try and kiss me again.' I drove away, leaving him standing alone on the side of the road.

'That was very forward of him,' says Ingrid. Today she is wearing those very big square dark glasses that accentuate the blondeness of her hair, her smooth matte make-up, her all in one black outfit. Leather boots, black tights, figure-hugging black jersey dress. Beside her on the chair in the café is her shiny black quilted jacket.

'I guess I knew what he wanted. Why else would someone his age make contact with me? He said he's learning salsa and tango. That's what attracted me.'

'You could go to dances with him and say he can dance with whoever he likes. But maybe you wouldn't like that.'

I shrug. 'Who knows?'

Ingrid settles herself back in the chair with a wiggle of her hips as she pushes herself firmly against the wall behind her. 'A friend of mine had the same experience. She met a bloke and everything seemed to go well. Then he sent her a message saying something about how he went all tingly when they said their goodbyes. They're all like that.'

Ingrid breaks a poached egg on top of the rye bread, uses a knife and fork to neatly manoeuvre the egg and the runny yolk that flows on top of the toast. The egg white drops off her fork as it nears her lips. A flick of her tongue and it's in her mouth. She places the second egg across the remaining toast like a bright yellow and white blanket and on top of that she piles a piece of bacon, folded in two.

Sometimes I just want to ignore what is staring me in the face. It's there with one hand tapping me on the shoulder but I just don't want to acknowledge its existence. But you know how it is? The future stretches out all grey and shapeless and more of the same, and you think, what the hell? Sometimes the best way to bring some colour and movement into your life is to grab a small piece and squeeze the bejeezus out of it.

Ingrid pulls out her wallet. Bits of paper fall out the sleeves of her purse as she puts it on the table, her diamond wedding ring catching a glint of the morning sun that has appeared between the Moreton Bay figs by the side of the beach.

She gets up, pulls her dress down at the sides, and stands in the small patch of winter sunshine as I make my way up the steps and into the café to pay.

The Festival

Brendan was sitting under one of those outdoor furnaces in front of a performance pavilion when I sat down beside him early on in the Music and Dance Festival. I hadn't realised it was him at first. I'd just ordered a coffee from the Italian joint that everyone seemed to like, maybe because of the heaters. Behind the counter the waitress, a slim, dark-haired pretty girl was calling the food orders through to the back. She wore a tangerine and emerald green scarf knotted at the front with a rose pinned at the side. Her freckled fingers were poised above a takeaway cup, pen in hand as she wrote the order on the side of the polystyrene.

When she called my name, I took my drink over to the spare chair beside a man who, though I didn't realise it at the time, was Brendan. It was the only free spot in the whole area. We started talking and realised we'd met before. Gone on a date even.

'Your face is familiar,' I said.

'You too. Where do we know each other from?'

We stayed at the plastic table sipping our drinks, a tall mug of hot chocolate for him, and a latte for me.

'I think we saw each other two or three times,' he said, cradling the mug with both hands.

I noted his bitten-down nails and eaten-off cuticles.

'Remember?' he said. 'We went for a walk in the park.'

'Oh, yeah. That's right.' I was eager to show I hadn't forgotten.

Behind and beside us were men and women on stilts and pogo sticks in among groups of performers in matching costumes of lederhosen with embroidered vests in between children on roller blades with intermittent fire-eaters and other circus performers. They milled around on the grass and along the streets that were filled with organic food stalls, instrument makers, furry animal-head hats on stands, clothes made of felt and velvet and suede, patchwork handbags, Celtic love rings, lace necklaces shaped like large bibs, freshly roasted almonds and magic fairy wands that cast a spell of watery bubbles. The sun shone and everything seemed highlighted by a bright light and it fell on my face with an unexpected warmth.

Our table was near the open flap of a performance marquee from which, now and then, a phrase or a lyric about love gone wrong floated our way from inside the tent.

I turned to Brendan, loosened the scarf from around my neck and removed my woollen beanie. He told me that I looked good, happier than when we'd last met. His blue checked shirt hung long over his trousers, his brown hiking boots were dusty. I assured him that he was looking pretty good himself, since that time a couple of years ago.

He asked if I wanted another coffee.

'Thanks all the same. But no.' I was rushing off to a drum workshop and didn't want to be late.

Brendan pulled a tin whistle out of his shoulder bag. He'd just been to a lesson. 'Would you like to hear a tune?' he asked.

'Naturally,' I said. 'Of course I would.'

I felt a certain lightness at having a few days off like that, enjoying a change of pace. The sunshine. The cloudless pale blue sky. The freedom of being there in that place and anonymous. The freedom too of being open to any eventuality, away from home and its comforting routines.

I was glad too that I had crossed paths with Brendan again. Always good to see a friendly face. Amanda was at the festival with Phoebe but I didn't expect to see much of them. They were all staying on-site in tents and I was in a motel within walking distance.

The budget motel, although past its heyday, was more than adequate, larger and less shabby than I remembered from last time. An avenue of pine trees led from the Federal Highway up to the reception area. From inside the room, or cabin, as the brochure called it, I could hear the rustling of the leaves on the trees.

The cabin was one room, up four steps from the driveway, a square box with kitchenette, fridge, toilet and shower. Outside the door, on the landing, pots of flowering cacti flourished, their last flash of the season. Against the wall at the foot of the double bed was a small table, on which I placed my laptop and an incense holder even though the sign on the front door said, 'No smoking or burning of candles in the cabins.'

I stood at the window, looking out past the cabins all in a row. Directly below there was a clothesline in the garden where a ginger-haired man was hanging out his laundry, underwear and shirts. Three pairs of fine black underpants, two striped shirts.

The autumn sun fell sideways into the yard, making the tarmac sparkle as if embedded with tiny diamonds. A young woman in a dark suit walked swiftly away across the driveway. Even from this distance, I imagined I could hear her stilettos clacking on the bitumen.

I first saw them, Peter and Sue, on that driveway on the first day on their way up to the festival. It was a warm windless morning. Peter was wearing jeans and a hooded top over a pale blue T-shirt on top of which were tufts of white hairy curls. On his head was clamped a grey felt fedora hat and over his shoulder a large round instrument bag. Sue, a petite, sandy-haired, not unattractive woman, wore a marquisette butterfly on the lapel of her big black wool coat which, in the warmth of the morning, gave off a barely discernible odour of stale smoke and spilt beer.

Peter and Sue took care to tell me, early on in the introductions, that they were sharing a room but weren't a couple. Sue asked how I occupied myself in the mornings. She said she walked up to the festival early because there was nothing much to do at the motel. I told her that I brought a couple of Sudoku books with me. Playing around with numbers relaxes me.

It was when I was waiting to go into a tango workshop that I first spotted Amanda. She was standing by the ladies' toilet block, shoulders hunched, using the arms of her parka as mittens. Instead of last year's black quilted down hiking jacket with the zip-off sleeves, she wore a new red number. The sun, making its way over the top of the pavilions, gave to her face a shiny youthful hue. I asked if she was coming into the lesson.

'No,' she said. 'Phoebe doesn't like to dance. We're going to drive into the city. Get away from here for a few hours.'

That's when Phoebe appeared, from the exit door of the toilets. I'd heard about her but we'd never met.

Amanda had emailed me to say, 'I suppose you know that I'm living in Balmain now?' She'd assumed that Ingrid had told me all the goss: that Amanda had met Phoebe and moved in after only a couple of weeks. First-time same-sex relationship for Amanda. And that they were thinking of either renovating, or buying a bigger place, to give each of them an office space.

Ingrid, who had introduced me to Amanda in the first place, said that we'd have to include Phoebe in everything now. 'Well, I'll have to,' Ingrid clarified, before turning to me. 'You don't have to, I suppose.'

It's not as if I'm an old friend. We'd had a lot of fun, the three of us, gossiping at the Crystal Ballroom about the other dancers and generally having a good old laugh. And, when necessary, we'd even shared the more sought-after of the dance partners – if we could get our hands on one of them.

'It's taking a bit of getting used to,' said Ingrid, 'seeing Amanda in this kind of a relationship.'

Anyway, I can't say I was particularly impressed with the sight of Phoebe when I did meet her. Plain and squat, her hair dyed the colour of liquorice and cut into a forest of uneven spikes, at attention on top of her head. She wore a cable-stitch cardigan in wide stripes of grey and cream over thick woollen leggings and off-white joggers secured with Velcro, branded with a lolly-pink tick.

But who was I to pass judgement on someone's personal style? It's not as if I looked anything wonderful, weighed down with backpack and drum bag and clumpy grandma shoes on my feet. I reminded myself to ask the pretty waitress how she tied her glamorous headscarf.

Phoebe might be a really nice person, though. I know they are both workaholics. They've got that in common. And Amanda seems happy enough, so why should I care? What's it to me who she spends her time with? None of my business what she does or doesn't do.

In the grassy area beyond the cabin stood a row of eucalypts, enormous actually, and a Hills hoist turning spasmodically in the wind. There were sheets and towels hung out to dry from the previous day that no one had brought in.

I stepped out the door of the room to the backyard. In between the wooden fence and a concrete path there was a garden of bromeliads shaded by the trees.

Perhaps it was the spell cast by the energy of the milling crowds, rather than the lethargy caused by long periods of inactivity sitting at my desk typing numbers on to a spreadsheet, that prompted me to try and accept the new situation of Amanda dating another woman.

I did not want the feeling of disappointment that came to me, which had been there all day, under the pulse of excitement, and which showed itself now in the way the sheets had been hung out, their edges in perfect lines, the towels in colour coordinated groups held fast on the line.

For several seconds, I was lost in the moment, looking down into that grassy place; especially at the eucalypts, their highest branches forced into movement by a cold breeze. A current of air flicked sheets and towels, shirts and socks, encouraging them to dance in the wind. Lighten up, I told myself. Lighten up. Amanda can do whatever she likes. Be with anyone she chooses.

It wasn't until I met up with Amanda and Phoebe in the big hall at the final concert that I saw them again. They'd saved me a seat. For the first-night concert, they'd saved me a seat too, but I was too exhausted to make the big trek up there from the motel. Maybe next year I'll hire a bike or a car. A forty-minute walk along the Federal Highway in the dark is very tiring. Up and back twice a day carrying all the gear: high-heeled dance shoes, a skirt, drum in bag, water bottle, extra layers of polar tech clothing. I'd said to Brendan how wearing it all is if you're not staying on-site in a tent. He said I could have a lie down in his tent of an afternoon if I didn't mind paying a small fee. Ha ha. At least this year they had some comfortable couches to recline on in one of the bars. But people would stretch out during the day and take up the whole space. Very annoying.

I was whingeing away to Peter and Sue about the logistics of it all, and they told me that there were lockers for instruments where you could leave your stuff in the day time so you didn't have to trek back to the motel to get a warm jacket or whatever. I had noticed Peter carrying his bodhran drum bag up each day and suspected he might carry a whole lot of gear in it. And now that I'd bought a new black bag for my bodhran, my round Irish frame drum that fitted neatly under my arm, I could do the same thing. But leaving the motel late morning and listening to bands all day and into the night was exhausting.

The light of afternoon felt murky and icy. A covering of clouds, curvaceous but oppressive, hung low above the pavilions.

We were there, Amanda, Phoebe and me at the final concert. I think Amanda and Phoebe were fighting. Phoebe wanted to go back to the tent before the finish of the show but Amanda preferred to stay on till the very end, like she usually does.

Up on the big concert stage, Kate Lovely sang with passion about her coffee obsession.

I said to Ingrid on the phone that I bet the relationship between Amanda and Phoebe ends after the festival. They've got nothing in common apart from sex and Amanda will get sick of Phoebe, I'm sure. Ingrid, Amanda's very oldest friend, said Amanda has never left the festival grounds before. She usually stays for the whole event and doesn't miss a second.

'We're very cosy in our tent,' Amanda had skited when I asked how they were coping with the below freezing night time temperatures.

'I heard that there was ice on the tents in the mornings,' I said.

'It makes a difference when you've got a warm body next to you,' Amanda grinned. 'Plus a good mattress and down jackets.'

So I never got to talk to the two of them, Amanda and Phoebe. They were head to head during the band changeovers. I didn't get a look in.

When I raced outside during a break to buy a Turkish gozleme from one of the food stalls for dinner, after one of the performance poets had done his thing – a long poem about longing and loss – there was Brendan again.

Night had fully fallen by now and in the flickering light of the outdoor furnaces the stalls lined up along the streets off into the darkness looked like caricatures from a circus, crazy shapes and cartoon hues of pink and purple and red and turquoise, incongruous against the bushy surrounds.

Brendan was approaching along the street, his head bowed and his arms folded across his chest and a hand clasped around a glass. He was bareheaded, and wore faded jeans, but was rugged up in scarf and thick jacket against the bitterly cold night. He opened his arms towards me.

'I'm off to get something to eat,' I said. I let my arms fall away.

He had no smell at all. No aftershave, no cleansing shampoo, no adornment.

'Just as well all the food stalls stay open till late,' I sighed.

He settled his eyes on me, both hands wrapped for warmth around his glass of hot wine. 'Exactly.'

'I keep buying things to eat,' I said.

He gave me a quick smile. 'So do I.'

'Food keeps me warm and happy,' I said in my jokey voice.

He crossed his arms again, as if holding himself up, then sighed, loud and full. 'Me too.'

A slant of moonlight fell along the street.

'Sometimes you just need to sigh,' Brendan said.

I nodded. 'To sigh out loud.'

Back in the motel room, the night had closed in. Everything had a softer, quieter look, like a series of lifeless images from a slide projector.

And there was that fly. He flew in from somewhere every day and landed on the kitchenette bench where the tea towel hung on the door of the melamine cupboard. He didn't sit for long, flying from one flat surface to another until he stopped. The buzzing fly circled, wings translucent before landing on the table.

The moon had misted over and there were no gusts of air to rouse the branches of the trees outside. But I could see there were other kinds of eucalypt out there, some with branches almost devoid of leaves, their trunks gnarled and twisted, precariously angled over the driveway. A tough species they must be, to survive the frosty nights.

The wind picked up, then changed direction. After no time at all, it had worked itself into a frenzy until it was blowing crazily, banging its knuckles against the ceramic urns on the landing on the other side of the door.

Ingrid

We had driven over to Balmain to see where Amanda was living with her new girlfriend, Phoebe. They'd told us there was no need to bring any food or drink. Just something to sit on. It's all a bit of a surprise, Amanda living with a woman. She's such a lover of men.

Anyway, Ingrid was trying to join in a conversation with Amanda and Phoebe under the downlights in the kitchen. I was watching from the adjacent open-plan dining room.

There was Ingrid standing there in those gorgeous cream lace leggings. She can get away with that sort of thing at her age because she's got great legs. Leggings, ivory voile over-shirt and a long off-white lace scarf. She's started wearing her blonde hair pulled back lately to show off dangly earrings that always look fabulous. And rows of bangles on each arm. Anyway, she'd removed herself from the table next to me, as we'd had an altercation during the main course. Not that anyone would have noticed.

The thing was, recently I'd driven past her jogging across a main road near a blind corner with her music plugged into her ears. So I'd commented that it looked dangerous, crossing near a blind corner with her ears plugged up.

That's when she'd shouted at me. 'Don't you think I've got eyes?' She covered her face to demonstrate. 'Do you think I'm blind?' She widened her eyes at me. 'What do you think I am? Stupid? I'm not stupid,' she repeated.

I gulped down my anger with a chilled white wine. It infuriated me when she went on like that. I turned away, trying to engage with Dennis on my left, but he was talking to Rose on his left.

'It is dangerous,' Ingrid admitted after a silence. 'But don't you ever walk listening to music?' She raised her chin in that defiant, determined way when she needs to show that she is right and you are wrong.

I glanced at her. 'I don't want to discuss it any more.'

She cupped her wine glass in her hand and sipped thoughtfully. After a moment, she asked loudly, 'Which are your favourite clothes shops these days?'

'I've got plenty of everything,' I said. 'You just need to mix and match differently and you've got a whole new outfit.'

Ingrid raised an eyebrow. 'I only buy on sale,' she declared with pride, waving her fork.

'Where did you buy those wonderful leggings?' I asked, as she sucked on a chicken bone.

'Sportsgirl. I love Sportsgirl.' She leaned back in her chair.

'Their windows always look amazing,' I said before picking up my drink and going outside to look at the balcony extension.

That's when Ingrid must have gone into the kitchen to join Amanda and Phoebe to talk about kitchen storage.

When Ingrid and Dennis headed for the front door, their fold-up chairs under their arms, I took another stale chocolate from the glass bowl.

I didn't turn round.

Aravind Again

Bacon and eggs. The smell wafts through from the kitchen and settles in the café like a cloying fog. Here I am, side by side with Ingrid and Amanda, drinking coffee.

I've told them Aravind has asked me to come for a visit. He's moved to Newcastle because he can't get a job in Sydney. He said I could come on a Thursday and we could dance Thursday, Friday and Saturday nights and go to the bowling club on the Sunday afternoon. Stay until Monday.

Amanda tips a half packet of sugar into her latte and stirs. 'Don't worry about Aravind's wife. Go for it. His wife lives in Sydney and he lives in Newcastle.'

Ingrid darts a wide-eyed look from Amanda to me. She spoons out the dregs of her flat white.

Amanda's smile is mischievous now. Without allowing for a pause for a rebuttal from Ingrid, she turns to me. 'You are going to visit him, aren't you, now he's invited you to come and stay?'

'He's got two bedrooms. He said I was welcome to sleep at his house, if I feel comfortable with that.'

It was late morning on a Saturday when I stood at the coach terminal in Newcastle, where the taxis line up, waiting for Aravind to pick me up. We had missed each other somehow, walked right past, so he rang me on the mobile to see where I was.

I am keen to tell Ingrid the whole story of what happened as we wait for the band to set up at the Crystal Ballroom. 'That was the first time I'd seen him dressed casually in shorts, T-shirt and a pair of walking sandals,' I tell her. 'Eccos, I think. Just like your Dennis wears.'

151

Ingrid shakes her head, her shoulders set high and tense. 'So you went to see him after all?'

I don't meet her gaze, but take a sip of my Kingfisher beer, and keep going with the story. 'Usually he's in his black ballroom trousers and a long-sleeved shirt. He opened the door for me to get into the car. It was parked right in front of me. That's what I mean. We must have walked right past each other. And you know what? His car is an Audi, not a BMW. It's got the four silver rings on the front and back. He said his other car has a cat on the front.'

'A Jaguar,' Ingrid puts in.

'That's one symbol I do know.'

Ingrid and I have settled ourselves in at a table near the front of the ballroom as people begin to fill the chairs that surround the circular tables. Dennis is upstairs playing the pokies.

The big band begins with Glenn Miller's 'In the Mood'. The trumpets, trombones and horns lead the way and a thrill rushes through my chest. Dancers in their evening wear, some in chiffon and satin and sequins, others in flounced skirts and sneakers, approach the floor. The chandeliers make a Goth-like contrast between the obligatory black of the clothing and the pale made-up faces. Quick steppers dance around the edges trying to avoid a collision with the swing dancers who take the middle of the floor.

'Hopefully, there won't be any altercations this evening – especially when I'm up there,' I say. 'I hate it when a dance partner gets angry with the other dancers or when someone tells you both off.'

'Exactly,' Ingrid agrees.

'That's what happened when I was dancing rock and roll with Aravind when I went to Newcastle. It was a very crowded dance floor with a live band. Four women were dancing together near us and twice they told Aravind off. "You can't dance rock and roll here," one said. "There's no room. Do you know you've already bumped into my friend?" I stood with my back to the women trying to ignore them between the brackets. It was a rock and roll band after all. They spoke with such venom that I wondered if they were racist, him being Indian.'

Ingrid lifts her eyebrows and sips her lemon, lime and bitters in unmistakable disapproval. 'What about his wife and children?'

'The children aren't children any more. They're grown-up. And they haven't even come to visit. It's been a year already. They call Newcastle a dump. He said they think most places are dumps. I asked where they would like to go. London or New York, he said.'

Ingrid stares into her drink and turns the glass.

'I stayed at a hotel, not far from the coach terminal,' I continue. 'Just for the one night. I wanted to check out the lie of the land before staying longer. And he's only got the one toilet. I thought that might be the case. He said that he's thinking of putting a second one into the laundry so when people come to stay it will make things easier. He showed me his room with its big double bed and an outlook on to some trees at the back of the block of units and then the second bedroom. White bedspread, his guitar under the bed. He must have tidied up before I came over.'

'Well, you would,' Ingrid states.

'Yes. If you'd invited someone over for dinner you'd tidy up before they arrived. It was pretty amazing, though, that he'd rung me as soon as I'd got on the coach from Sydney to say he'd like to have me over, either for lunch, or for dinner before we went out to the dance. I was very surprised.'

Ingrid blinks, sips her drink. 'I don't give advice and I don't want other people giving me advice.' She shrugs and sips again. 'Just give me the details.'

I keep going. 'I said to him on the phone, "What a nice person you are."'

'"Is there anything you don't like to eat?" he asked. "I'm about to go out and do the shopping."

'In my rush to assure him that I eat anything, anything would be fine, I forgot to say I'm not crazy about seafood, apart from fish of course, and that I don't eat dairy. So I had my fingers crossed, and toes, when he served up a seafood chowder and garlic bread and a very oily fatty salad, forgot to say I can't digest fat, and I worried all night that I'd get another allergic reaction to the calamari. But it was okay. He was so proud of himself for having made dinner for me.

'"My first time," he said with a big grin. "Now I know I can do it."

'Thank God I didn't vomit it all up. Anyway, it was very touching. When he almost insisted I have another piece of the microwaved garlic bread. I had to say, "I don't usually eat garlic when I go out dancing."

'"Don't worry," he assured me, sticking his tongue out like a dragon. "We've both eaten it."'

Ingrid's gaze settles on me for an extended second, a pause just long enough to show she's absorbed what I've said but she won't be drawn into putting her thoughts into words.

'He'd picked me up from my hotel,' I continue. 'And when we walked in to his unit, the food was already on the plates that were set up on the table. He took the plates to the microwave one at a time to warm them up.'

'So what was his place like?' Ingrid asks.

'Very small. The little balcony off the lounge dining area looks out on to a brick wall. He likes it, though. Seemed very proud. I asked him if his wife had helped choose it. She had. "What do you usually eat?" I asked when I realised he didn't usually cook a meal.

'"You'll laugh," he said. "But I buy these frozen dinners and just heat them up." He went to the freezer and pulled one out to show me.

'He'd seated me at the head of the table and he sat opposite, down the other end. In the middle was the large meat and cheese salad and the bowl of garlic bread.'

I tip some more beer into my glass and take a sip before going on with the story. Out on the dance floor in front of us, Natalie, the band leader, has stepped up to the microphone. Her voice issues meltingly from the stage in a rendition of 'It Had To Be You'. The dancers are up close in couples, working together with their bodies in the backward flow of the foxtrot.

I turn to Ingrid and drop back into the telling of what happened.

'Aravind had decorated the unit totally in white and green. I'd asked him if that meant he had lots of pot plants.

'"No," he said. "Just imitation plants."

'"Oh no," I said. "Imitation plants get very dusty."

'"So do the real ones," he said.

'Anyway, he had a small glass desk against one wall and wanted to buy a green or a white office chair. He seemed very proud of his colour scheme. The green leather lounge was one of five that he'd brought from the family home in Sydney.

'"You're not going to stay here forever are you?" I asked when he told me about some of his decorating ideas.

'"Why not?" he said. "I might."'

Ingrid clanks her glass down then rolls an elastic band off her wrist and ties her blonde hair in a ponytail on the top of her head. She's dressed in a red flounced skirt and flat shoes ready to practise the new swing routine that she and Dennis have learnt. Her hair ready, she folds her arms and leans towards me. 'It must be hard for him living away from his family.'

'He did it before for three years. That's why he knows he can do it again in Newcastle.'

'So?' Ingrid sips her drink, sips it again and looks at me. 'Did anything happen?'

'Not much. He hadn't rung either of the clubs to check if the band was playing on the Saturday night. They weren't. We drove around Newcastle in the pouring rain and had to keep getting out of the car into the wet. Not much fun. Anyway, we ended up at some club way out of town. No proper dancing.'

Ingrid blinks. 'No proper dancing? You mean you went all the way to whoop-whoop and didn't even get to dance?'

'We bopped away to a live band but there was no eye contact between us. He watched the tennis on a video screen on the wall. I kept changing my position so his line of vision was altered, but he seemed to be able to see a video screen from each side of the dance floor.'

Ingrid sniggers.

I'm remembering when the band had begun to play a ballad from Nicolette Larson, a piece I loved so much to rumba to. A dreamy song that made me want to beg him to sweep me away in its sensuality. But Aravind looked right past me the whole time, disconnected. He wouldn't take me to the core of the music and suddenly I felt stupid for going all that way to visit him and for letting the soppy sentimental mood of the rumba overwhelm me. I don't say any of this to Ingrid.

'Don't laugh at me, Ingrid,' I say. 'Don't be a mean bitch.' I say this matter-of-factly, as though there should be absolutely nothing wrong with me going to see Aravind. 'At the end of the night, he drove me back to my motel and walked me to my room. I didn't ask him in. Why would I? He hadn't even looked at me on the dance floor.'

'You didn't want to be rejected,' Ingrid declares. She reaches across the table in a maternal manner and pats the back of my hand.

'I really don't understand what the story is with him,' I say, after a pause. 'Maybe it's a cultural thing. Different cultures.'

She gives a considered nod, like someone checking the list of ingredients on a packet at the supermarket. 'Indian men don't know how to romance a woman. They're used to having their relationships arranged for them. They think Western women are going to come along and sweep them off their feet and drag them away.'

I laugh and take another sip of my cold beer. 'The funny thing is that when we went for a coffee the next morning after the Saturday night and I was in the ladies' room and came back out, he told me the waitress had been very chatty. She asked him what we did last night. He told her we'd had a fantastic night. I was pretty surprised when he said that. A fantastic night. What I remember is that there was a lot of sitting in silence.'

'A friend of mine used to counsel a woman who was married to an Indian man and they're very close to their families,' Ingrid says waving her straw. 'They don't leave their wives. But you wouldn't want to get married again, would you?'

'Having sex with someone changes everything. I'd be happy to leave it at the dancing.'

'Yeah, right.'

'It's true.'

The band starts up again with 'Chattanooga Choo Choo' and, as the music swells, the dance floor fills. The dancers stride, glide or spin by.

Ingrid glances at her watch, gasps, 'Time is marching on. When are we going to get a dance? Where's Dennis?'

I shrug, anxious to finish the story. 'Aravind rang his wife on his car phone when he was driving me back to the coach station on the Sunday. He wanted some advice from her about trying to get out of a dinner with some friends of theirs who were visiting Newcastle. His wife told him not to go if he didn't want to. He complained that all they wanted to do was sit around and eat. He told his wife that I was in the car and he was dropping me back to the coach station. "Who?" his wife asked. "Sofia," he repeated. Then he handed the phone over to me and I had to speak to her. It was all very awkward.'

Ingrid leans over the table towards me. 'He just wants to be friends, that's all.' Her tone is impatient now. 'I told you before, Sofia, Indian men never divorce their wives.'

'Yes, you always know best, Ingrid.' My tone catches on resentment but I laugh. 'I should know that by now. I should listen to what you tell me.'

The band has begun to play 'Let's Fall in Love' when Dennis enters and is spotted by Ingrid, who waves at him across the room. He saunters up carrying a plastic cup full of peanuts.

'There you are,' says Ingrid.

Dennis plonks the container on the table, then grabs Ingrid's wrist and leads her out to the floor. He steers her through the mass of dancers. I startle when there's a tap on my shoulder from behind.

A man extends his hand. 'Follow me,' he says. He squeezes my fingers gently.

That's the thing. It's just like I've always said. It's the excitement of not knowing. The possibility that something unexpected might happen.

Libby Sommer's debut novel *My Year With Sammy*, published by Ginninderra Press in December 2015, was *The Sydney Morning Herald* Spectrum's Pick of the Week in January 2016 and was awarded the Society of Women Writers Fiction Book Award 2016.

Libby Sommer grew up in Sydney. After leaving school at the age of fifteen, she worked at a variety of jobs until securing a position as part-time relief typist at ABC television. Within twelve months she was promoted to a full-time position as assistant producer on dramas and documentaries.

A single parent with three children, she waited until the children grew up before she tipped them out of the nest, joined Youth Hostels, threw on a backpack and headed off to Europe for two years of discovery and adventure.

She'd always dreamt of becoming a writer. On her return to Australia, she enrolled at university as a mature-age student and graduated with an MA in Professional Writing in 2001. Since then, more than thirty of her short fictions have been published in Australia and internationally. Her poetry appears in Australian anthologies and literary magazines. She is the recipient of a Varuna Fellowship and was shortlisted and highly commended for the D.J. O'Hearn Fellowship (Melbourne University) and twice shortlisted for a Varuna/Harper Collins Award for Manuscript Development. She won the UTS Short Short Story Competition and was shortlisted for the Canberra National Short Story Competition (Canberra University), Seizure's Viva La Novella Competition and MsLexia Memoir Competition.

Libby Sommer lives in Sydney but escapes to a small fishing village in the south of France as often as possible. She loves to dance the tango.

Blog: www.libbysommer.wordpress.com